Looking for it

USA TODAY BESTSELLING AUTHOR

ALLYSON LINDT

To every geek girl,
everywhere,
trust yourself.

Chapter One

Things I didn't know I didn't want to see until I saw them:

How hot dogs are made.

The Black Friday line at Walmart.

My brother's best friend, in my bedroom, with my vibrators and other assorted toys scattered at his feet.

Jax had been around almost as long as I could remember—hanging out with my brother since they were in kindergarten and I was a year too young to join them. There was a span of time when he wasn't welcome, but since we'd made things right, I didn't mind having Jax around. With his short brown hair, piercing hazel eyes, and a physique that didn't need a rubber suit to show off the definition, seeing him— the looking—was fantastic.

"Who knew little Dee Dee had a wicked side?" A smirk tugged up one corner of his mouth.

No one else had called me *Dee Dee* since high school, nearly a decade ago. It was *Sadie*, or *Mercedes* if the occasion was formal. But sometimes when Jax said it, I could pretend it was a pet name, and not just a long-time habit.

"Anyone who's watched the outtakes on her Patreon." Grayson's voice came from behind me.

He was referring to one arm of my business. I made costumes based on characters from video games, movies, and whatever else caught my eye. Usually anime. It was why my short hair was currently lavender. My last outfit had been Ayane from Dead or Alive. YouTube let me share how-to videos, print-on-demand gave me a way to sell books, and Patreon let the fans support my hobby. In exchange, they got access to some of the sillier, more sweary outtakes from my vids.

Jax tapped his chin. He perpetually had two days' worth of stubble on his face. I swore, even right after he shaved? Stubble. "Those are probably my favorites. Closest we get to seeing the real Sadie."

I crossed the short distance to Jax and took the broken cardboard box from his hands. "I've got this. Thanks." I tried to keep my tone even. To pretend I wasn't utterly embarrassed by the assortment of battery-operated latex toys on the carpet.

I was moving today, and my brother was supposed to help me. He had to take a last-minute weekend meeting with a client and asked Jax to step in. Since Jax was dating Grayson, and Grayson had

looking for it

the pickup truck to haul most of my stuff, that meant I got both guys for the price of one.

I liked Grayson's company too. His wit. How incredible he looked in the cosplay armor I designed. His mind, of course.

At least it wasn't my brother who picked up the less-than-secure box of toys. I shoved them back in their temporary home. I'd used more than one of these when I fantasized about being with Grayson. Or Jax. Or both. They liked to invite other people into their bed and share, and my imagination liked me being that person.

While I personally couldn't imagine loving sharing someone with another person, my mind could run a marathon with the idea of being with both men at the same time. My favorite accessory was probably the U-shaped toy, with the textured end that slid inside me, and the suction end that vibrated against my—

"I'll help." Jax's hand brushed over mine when he knelt next to me, and sparks danced along my skin. "These are a lot of fun with a partner."

I— What? He had to be teasing me. A glance showed his expression was playful.

"I have them for when there *isn't* another person." I could do this. I could talk about sex toys with a straight face. Without giggling like a kid. The heat flooding my face said I must be tomato red by this point, but I wasn't backing down.

"So you've never done it?" Jax asked.

Grayson cleared his throat. The sound was loud and exaggerated.

Good. He could shut his boyfriend down.

Jax glanced at him. "Sadie and I are having an adult conversation. If she doesn't like it, she can say so."

Do it. Tell him now to stop.

Or let him keep going, and see if he blinked first. Everything he said was going in the Fantasy Pile, and imagining the two of them helping me masturbate was a pretty good addition.

"*Done it?* As in *sex*? Are we twelve? No. I'm not a virgin." Wow. I actually said that without my voice cracking.

"Not that, gorgeous." Another nickname that always meant more to me than it probably should, coming from him. He had a way of making it sound sincere and light-hearted at the same time. Jax held up a bullet vibrator. "Played with one of these with someone else."

The fantasies existed because I didn't have many memories of good sex. Not that my love life was all bad; it just wasn't toe-curling, sheet-clutching, back-scratching amazing. That kind of thing was for the imagination and porn. "No."

looking for it

"I'd be willing to give you a demonstration."

He was taking this a lot further than I expected. And what was I supposed to make of Grayson's silence?

I was going to see how far Jax ran with this idea. If the answer *all the way*, I still wasn't flinching first.

Who was I kidding? I loved every minute of it. Desire hummed through my veins, and the heat under my skin was as much need as it was embarrassment.

There was a big, gaping flaw in his proposal, besides the fact that I shouldn't even flirt with my brother's friends, let alone consider fucking one of them. "If it's all toys, even with a second person, is it really sex?" I asked.

"If it's not, you've got the wrong second person," Jax said.

Of course. "What about you?" I looked at Grayson. "Are you just going to stand there and watch?"

He shrugged. "Sometimes. In this case, I'm thinking *yes*."

Because their relationship was open. Adding the idea of Grayson, watching, to that of getting a taste of Jax drove my senses wild, and it was probably status quo for them.

It was a bad idea, for me to even pretend I could live in that part of their world, regardless of what the tingles racing through me wanted.

Apparently, I was going to blink first. "Lyn's waiting on us. We should finish packing up the cars."

I shoved the box of toys on my dresser, to grab last. This way, I could keep it in the front seat with me and make sure that tonight, when I fantasized about giving Jax a different answer, I had latex help on hand.

We resumed loading boxes—bigger and heavier ones in Grayson's truck, and smaller in my car.

I was moving into a spare bedroom, in my best friend's house. Lyn owned a corner lot shop she'd purchased for a steal at a foreclosure auction. She turned the main floor into a gaming café, complete with a bakery for her own sinfully amazing baked goods.

A few months ago, she did a massive remodel on the shop—fiber optics in the walls. High-end gaming chairs, top-of-the-line hardware, and her dream kitchen for producing mass quantities of sweets. Business slowed for her right after, and she was struggling to pay back the loan for the overhaul.

My lease was up and I needed a month-to-month deal until the jobs I was pursuing in L.A. panned out, but my living with Lyn would also help her make ends meet until things picked up again for her business.

looking for it

I grabbed one of the last boxes from my bedroom and was heading outside, when I found Grayson in the living room. He'd taken my replica lightsaber from its cradle, a grin on his face.

"*Power.* Unlimited *power.*" He held the lightsaber above his head, and called out in his best Palpatine voice.

The replica had been a gift from him and Jax. I was on a Star Wars kick after *The Force Awakens* came out, and they gave it to me to accent my Rey costume. The only thing that made the gift more perfect was I had no idea they'd made the purchase when I'd gotten them each one too, as a *thank you* for Jax's being my Kylo Ren and Grayson's being my Poe.

I took the weapon from him. "So this is how liberty dies. With thunderous applause." The game was simple. Pick a quote from a series, and each person had to add onto it with another—not necessarily the right one.

"Count me outta dis one." Jax's high-pitched Jar Jar Binks impersonation came from behind. He rested a hand on the small of my back as he stepped around me, and warmth spread out from his touch.

It was a simple gesture, to let me know he was here, and one he'd made countless times in the past. Today, it sparked images that weren't ready to be shoved aside.

"Apparently, you left a lot of your toys out," Jax said.

"I wanted to make sure this one travelled safely. It's special and doesn't go in a box." It was tempting to say something more about the *toy* comment, but I needed to let that line of conversation die.

Even if my mind was taking Jax's hand on the small of my back and spinning it into a rom-com style hookup. Except, instead of an awkward kiss that ended in light laughs, the next step was Jax, lifting me onto the kitchen counter and fucking me until I screamed.

I mentally shook myself and got back to work. Now wasn't the time. I never had an issue separating fantasy from reality before. Then again, Jax never offered to help me play with my vibrator while Grayson watched before.

He'd only been teasing, to see how I'd react. My *no* ended the moment, as it should have, and it was time to let things go.

I climbed onto the bed of Grayson's truck, to settle a box in among the others. It was like Tetris, but sweatier. When I stepped back toward the edge, Grayson was waiting his turn. He reached up and grabbed my hips, to help me hop down.

Which was perfectly normal and nothing to get excited about.

looking for it

"I think we're almost done," he said. "Want to do one last pass?"

"Yeah. Good call." I headed back into the house, and surveyed each room carefully. All of the boxes were gone. Every loose item I wanted to keep an eye on was secured in my car. Only furniture was left.

Last stop was my bedroom. I paused just inside the doorway, using the silence to collect my thoughts. I was about to make some huge changes in my life, and my mind spent its free time these days going over all the details again and again.

The lack of certainty in the rest of my life was the only reason Jax's playful offer wouldn't leave me alone. There was no other explanation for the excitement that thrummed under my skin at the thought of his hands, roaming over me. His lips. His everything.

No other explanation at all.

And the brief conversation about sex toys was no reason to let things become long-term awkward with my brother's friends. *My* friends.

I heard the front door close, and footsteps echoed through the apartment.

Jax stopped behind me, one hand on my back again. Even without the familiar gesture, I always knew it was him. His cologne was faint but distinct, and currently adding another level of reality to my fantasies.

"I wasn't joking." His voice was throaty. Intoxicating.

"About what?" I knew what, but I needed to hear him say it.

He moved his hands to my hips and pointed me toward the box on my dresser. The one I'd almost overlooked, and would have been super disappointed to find missing when I got to my new place.

"You're not the least bit curious?" he asked.

"Maybe." The answer slipped out without my permission. "But talk about making things awkward."

"It doesn't have to." Grayson had joined us.

The images surged in full force. Not just of Jax. Now Grayson watched us…

Desire sparked in my gut and spread through my limbs.

"We're all adults," Jax said. "This doesn't have to be a big deal." Did his voice catch?

No. That was my breath, hitching at the implication. Could I really do casual sex *with them*? Probably. I never had a problem looking either of them in the eye after fingering myself to visions of one of them going down on me while I sucked the other off. "Good point."

looking for it

Jax turned me to face him and cupped my cheek. I could drown in those liquid-amber eyes. "I'll ask you directly, one more time. You tell me to drop it, and I'll never bring it up again. Are you interested in a hands-on demonstration of how much fun a toy can be with a partner?"

Yes. *God* yes. I should say *no*, but if I did, I'd regret passing up this chance for a long time.

"All right. Show me." My pulse hammered in my ears so loudly I barely heard myself speak. "Let's have some casual fun." Why did I add that last bit?

Jax's raised eyebrow echoed my question, but he rested his other hand on my cheek and brushed his mouth over mine.

The feather-light touch sent a million tiny jolts through me, and I gasped. How did he do that with just a kiss?

He glided his hand to the back of my neck, gripped my hair, and crushed his lips to mine. This kiss was hard. Demanding. He danced his tongue around mine in a hungry tango.

I planted my palms on his chest, to keep my balance, and fisted his T-shirt, gripping as though my life depended on it. A whimper escaped my throat.

Jax pulled away with a self-satisfied smirk.

I liked it. "That had *nothing* to do with a vibrator." My voice was breathy, and my head swam.

"I didn't see any lube." He grasped my fingers. "So it's either packed away, or you don't need it. Personally, I always imagined you with a sloppy wet pussy, but either way, I have to make sure you're nice and slick."

He'd imagined me...? I was definitely wet after a kiss and a line like that.

Chapter Two

Jax trailed his finger down my neck so lightly, shivers raced down my spine.

I could remind him about the toys, but if his goal was to turn me on and make me slick, it was working.

He followed a different path back up, to brush my ear and then my jaw. My mouth parted in a silent sigh, and he drew his finger along my bottom lip. I pulled him in with my tongue. The twin groans that greeted me were intoxicating, and the reminder that Grayson was watching hammered in my ears to the beat of my pulse.

Jax moved his other hand to my breast, to tease through the heavy fabric of my sweatshirt. He brushed a thumb over my nipple, and the soft fleece tickled my sensitive skin. He kept up the attention until I was squirming and squeezing my thighs together.

"Let's see if you're ready." He undid my jeans and glided his hand over my panties. Dampness had to be seeping through. With a dangerously sexy grin, he shoved my pants and underwear to the floor, rested his hands on my hips, and guided me back to lie on my bed. "Don't move."

It was awkward being naked from the waist down, on a bare mattress, with two men in my room. But he wasn't gone long enough for me to dwell on the thought. Jax held up a vibrator—my current favorite—and turned it on.

I reached for it.

"Hands off," he ordered, "unless you want me to bind them."

That was tempting. "I can't just lie here."

"You can, but if you need something to do, play with your breasts." Jax shoved my sweatshirt up to my neck.

I hesitated. Being on display? Not new. Doing so completely exposed, while one guy stroked himself through his jeans and the other teased me with a vibrator? The situation shouldn't be so tantalizing.

I did as he ordered, cupping my boobs and pinching my nipples the way I would if I were drawing out a personal-play session.

Jax paused, to free himself from his jeans and roll on a condom. "Don't want to forget in heat of the moment."

Why did using toys require him to wear a condom?

looking for it

The question evaporated when he slid the vibrating head along my slit. I gasped at the rush of pleasure. He followed the same path a few times, brushing my clit but never lingering. My hips thrust on their own, needing more… everything.

When he finally slipped the toy inside me, I groaned at the penetration. He teased with both ends of the device, pushing me close to orgasm, then backing away each time my breath grew shorter.

He finally pressed the suction end to my clit, and I clenched around the device as I climaxed.

When Jax slid inside me, next to the vibrator instead of withdrawing it first, I cried out. *Oh God.*

The twin sets of pressure, him sliding back and forth, and it staying mostly in place, drew out my pleasure until bright lights sparked behind my eyelids.

I heard a duet of grunts, Jax and Grayson, but I was too lost in sensation to focus on either. I was pretty sure the vibrator slipped out, but I didn't care. Not with the way Jax slammed inside me, his pelvis rocking against mine and his cock hitting me at the perfect angle.

His groans grew tighter as his movements became more frantic, then a pause and a shudder. He gripped my hips tight, and released, I knew he came too.

Jax dropped to his elbows, barely holding himself above me. The heat of his chest mingled with mine. He dipped his head, mouth near my ear. "*God, Dee Dee, you're incredible.*" His voice was so soft, I could have imagined the words. His breath on my skin said this was all real.

The desire to giggle like a little girl was back. I settled for a quiet, "You too."

"I think you're both pretty fucking amazing." Grayson's voice was strained. I rolled my head to the side, to see him with his dick in his slick, glistening hand. *Fuck.* He came to the sight of us.

This was better than any fantasy.

The opening strains of "Heathens" by Twenty One Pilots filtered through the room—usually one of my favorite sounds, because it meant one of my best friends was calling. "I should get that. It's probably Lyn." I couldn't keep the disappointment from my voice.

"Yeah." Jax slipped out of me and pushed to his feet. He grabbed my phone from my nightstand and handed it over.

I stared the way his jeans hung off his hips, his softening cock dangling loose. I mentally shook my head and answered the phone. "Hey."

"You all right?" Lyn asked. "You sound winded."

looking for it

"Moving boxes does that." I'd probably spill the beans about this as soon as she and I were alone, but it felt awkward right now. In fact, a whole lot of uncomfortable was setting in. How was I supposed to act around Jax and Grayson?

"Good point," Lyn said. "Anyway, you were taking a while, so I called to make sure you were okay. See if you needed me to send the troops. Or a hot pizza guy."

I definitely didn't need the second one. The guys left my room, and the sound of running water came from the bathroom. "I'm good. Chase couldn't make it, so we made other arrangements. But I'm on my way soon, and I'll explain everything when I get there." The drive should give me a chance to figure out what *everything* was.

"A line like that, and I expect a story."

A story. "It's not a big deal." Understatement of the year. "See you soon."

The guys reappeared, both dressed again. Jax lingered in the doorway, watching me with an unreadable expression. Grayson sat next to me on the bed.

I tugged my sweatshirt down, suddenly intensely aware that I was still half-naked.

"Are we good?" Grayson's arm brushed mine.

Good? They were incredible. It didn't matter that he hadn't touched me. That he got off to the show made it that much hotter. But that wasn't what he meant. He wanted an assurance that nothing had changed between the three of us.

"We're good," I said.

He kissed me on the forehead—a gesture that had never seemed more than friendly until this moment. "We'll see you there."

"And we should keep this between us," Jax said from the doorway.

Grayson frowned.

My warm fuzzies vanished. Of course they'd want discretion. Why would Jax want anyone to know he'd done anything with me? "Of course." My tone was cool. "I'm not telling anyone."

Jax clenched his jaw.

"That's not how he meant it." Grayson's voice was hard.

How many ways were there to mean *don't tell anyone we had sex?*

"Forget it." Jax jerked his head toward the front door. "Let's go."

Chapter Three

After a quick cleanup of my own, and a touch-up to my makeup and hair to get rid of that *freshly fucked* look, I was on my way to Lyn's.

I shouldn't be irritated about Jax's request. It wasn't like I thought that one moment would lead to more. Their future involved the two of them, and mine pointed toward a Hollywood career, a doting husband, an amazing wedding, and the most perfect dress anyone had ever seen.

But I didn't like the idea of being anyone's dirty little secret. That stung. It hurt worse that Grayson put up so little argument, than Jax's making the request in the first place.

I cracked the window in my ancient Subaru, to let the cold December air hit my hot face. I loved this time of year. Yeah, I was a Basic Girl. Uggs and Peppermint Mochas all the way. Most people expected me to love Halloween the most, but I dressed up year-round—bonus to being a cosplay queen. The only thing that made October different was everyone else did as well.

Some people said costumes were about pretending to be someone else for a night or two. In a way, I agreed. But it was more about embracing individuality. Not pretending I was someone else, but being me, in whatever package, job, and universe I chose. I loved to see people exploring that. Which was the reason I loved Christmas. For me, it was all about finding the perfect gift for each person.

The holiday lights were gorgeous too. I could wander for hours through a Christmas village, admiring the lights and losing myself in the cheery mood.

When I got settled in my new place, I had big plans for Christmas activities on my channel. Things like quick accessories and unique gifts for anime fans that anyone could make from supplies around the house. How to go from safe-for-work Christmas cheer to sexy-fun after with the same outfit. Grayson was even going to model the guys' stuff for me.

Would he still agree? How much had our friendship changed? Not at all?

I didn't believe that. Neither did they. *We should keep this between us*. Jax's voice was back in my head, taunting me.

Jax's mother was sick a lot while we were growing up, which made him a semi-permanent fixture in our house. By the time I reached junior high, I'd decided I was going to marry him when we

looking for it

grew up. Which was how I got into sewing, and then cosplay. The perfect wedding required the ultimate dress, and I didn't trust anyone else to make mine for me. Not that I ever told him any of that. Thank God.

Back then, I was certain our love was meant to be, and he'd figure it out sooner rather than later. I was such an idiot, but not in the *I should have approached him* sort of way. In high school, things changed. I hit my junior year, and Jax got friendly. He'd always been nice, but this was different. He started flirting. I ate it up.

There were rumors he was going to ask me to the New Year's dance, and I was figuring out what kind of dress I was going to make. Satin. Blue, to match my eyes. Gold ribbon and embroidery to match his.

Thinking about how naive I'd been clenched like a fist around my heart. Chase had stopped me before I spent an entire paycheck on fabric. He was so nice and sympathetic, and that didn't make his words any easier to hear. Jax had been bragging— locker room talk—about how awesome he was. He'd convinced the girl in the tacky outfits that he liked her.

Chase promised me he'd shut Jax down. Said no one could talk about his sister like that.

Jax hadn't stopped flirting, though. Nausea churned in my gut, at the reminder of his asking me to that dance. I'd told him—screamed in the middle of the school common area—that I wanted him to stop. I wouldn't be his joke.

He did stop. Stopped talking to both Chase and me. Stopped coming to the house. I still hurt over the entire thing. The day they graduated, he *apologized.*

I'm sorry. For whatever I did. I didn't mean it.

It took a few years, but I forgave him enough to be friendly with him. He and Chase made up sometime in college, and we all grew up and moved on. It had been a decade, and the way we got along now allowed me to separate that moment from him.

Today wasn't a mistake. I'd had fun. As far as I could tell, they did too. However, I needed to distance myself from what happened, the way I did with our past.

Which started now, since I was at Lyn's place, and she was helping Jax and Grayson carry in my boxes from Grayson's truck.

Fortunately, this part didn't require much interaction. Grab some stuff, take it up to my new room on the second floor, and go back for the next load. I swore the process took longer than loading the vehicles had.

As we moved the last few boxes, I worked on pasting a smile into place. The manual labor had pushed most of my muddled-brain-ness aside, as well as chasing away the winter chill.

looking for it

I grabbed a couple of lighter tubs that stacked, and headed for the stairs, passing Lyn. She spun on her toe, fell into step beside me, and tugged the back of my hair.

"Ow." It didn't hurt so much, as caught me off-guard. "What was that for?"

She held up a piece of fuzzy lint, the same color as my mattress pad. "Love the new accessory. Are we calling this *Catch of the Day?*"

"I wasn't *catching* anything." I snagged the fluff from her hand and shoved it in my pocket. "That's what condoms are for." We were eternally teasing each other about our sex lives. I shouldn't have dropped the hint that she was right this time. Not while Jax and Grayson were here. Not after that exchange earlier.

"No shit. Is this why you took so long?"

At three-quarters excited and three-quarters confused, I was bursting to share. "Maybe."

"Since when are you seeing someone. Are you? Did you send Mr. Mysterio home before they showed up, or is he why Jax is scowling?" Lyn spoke quietly, but excitement hummed in her voice. She was about half a second from peppering me with questions so quickly I wouldn't be able to keep up. "Did they interrupt you?"

"No. That definitely wasn't an issue." There was no way I wasn't blushing. I set my load on top of an existing stack. This room was as big as my old bedroom and living room combined. The flat-white walls in here were going to be so much better for filming against when the occasion called for it.

I turned to see Lyn, staring at me with wide eyes, her mouth agape. "No shit," she said.

"We need your keys." Grayson's voice came from the doorway, both startling me and sending a pleasant shiver up my spine.

I whirled to face him, digging the ring out of my pocket. Did he overhear us? He was watching me with a strange expression, but it almost looked... sad. Or was that longing? Definitely not. "For what?" I asked.

"The rest of your stuff is in the hallway. We're going to grab a truck full of your furniture."

"Sounds good. I'll meet you there."

He held out his hand. "We'll do this run alone. It's really only a two-person job."

"Oh. Okay." I couldn't keep the hurt from my voice as I handed him the keys to my apartment. It was a reasonable request, but it felt like there was more attached to it.

Grayson dipped his head next to my ear, and a flash of memory overlapped Jax and that tender moment earlier. "It's okay. I promise," Grayson whispered. "We'll talk this afternoon."

looking for it

I nodded and stepped back. "Text me when you leave there, and we'll order pizza."

I watched him until he disappeared around a corner and down the stairs. Normally, I'd be enjoying the view, but my mind was in other places.

"Oh. My. Lord." Lyn's exclamation dragged me out of my head. "Does Grayson know? Or was it with him? That's why Jax is upset—he walked in on you. No. You said you weren't interrupted. Was it both of them? *Holy shit*, what was that like? What were you thinking? Chase is going to flip. Not that it's any of his business. Was it amazing? I bet it was. *Tell me.*"

A tiny laugh escaped me, mingled with a sigh. Lyn was a literal genius, and her brain and mouth tended to lay out everything all at once, rather than pondering any of it first.

I was a master of acting without thinking everything through, but she thought it as she did it. When I met her I didn't know how to process her behavior. Now I adored it.

"It was amazing. And confusing. They were both there." I wasn't ready to share details. If I talked about it, the magic might vanish, and I was already struggling with the fallout. "What was I thinking?"

"You were thinking you were tired of being trapped in a *shoujo*, where there's so much tension you think the room might explode, and you wanted to finally move past the final end credits and do more than gaze longingly at each other." Lyn grabbed my hand and tugged me toward the kitchen.

I rolled my eyes, but her enthusiasm was chasing away my dread. "We're not an anime. It was a one-time thing. There's no *happily ever after* here." For them, maybe. And for me separately, with my one and only guy.

"You say that now." She handed me a Mt. Dew and grabbed herself a Diet Coke from the fridge.

We took seats at the kitchen table. "Forever. I'm not supposed to tell anyone. They're embarrassed about it. I made a mistake, didn't I?"

"Does it *feel* like a mistake? Not the circles your brain is chasing you in, but the actual moment. Do you want to take it back?"

I wanted the awkwardness around it to go away, but not at the cost of... Yeah, I wasn't ready to give up the memory of Jax's touch. His kisses. Grayson's gaze on us. His groans. "No."

"So it wasn't a mistake. They're big boys; they can deal with it. They *are* big, aren't they?"

My laugh was back. "I'll never tell."

"Yes, you will." Lyn kicked me under the table. "And that's all the answer I need."

Thank God for friends who got me. If only what came next—talking through things with Grayson and Jax—was going to be even a fraction as simple.

Chapter Four

Jax and Grayson returned with my bed strapped to the bed of Grayson's truck and the rest of my bedroom set underneath. Most of my furniture was going into storage or to my other best friend, Anne, since Lyn already had furniture here.

Seeing the guys bring my bed in summoned memories of the last thing we'd done on it, and a knot formed in my gut. Fortunately, the arrival of the pizza lady was the perfect distraction.

Lyn and I gathered sodas and stacks of plates from her upstairs kitchen. She always had a massive variety of drinks on hand, because she got a good deal buying them in bulk for the shop. I was grateful when she suggested we set it all up on the coffee table in the living room. I still needed to figure out simple things like, could I make eye-contact with Grayson and Jax? The kitchen table would make that a more pressing concern than I was prepared to deal with.

When Lyn grabbed a small salad from the fridge, I frowned. "It's moving day. Indulge." I kept my tone light.

Lyn was gorgeously curvy, and every other month she started another diet to hide her amazing features. "Burning calories isn't an excuse to consume more."

"That's exactly what it is." I wished I could make her see what I did—that her intelligence and beauty didn't need to bend to fit anyone else's perspective. She was perfect as-is. I wouldn't push the issue today, though.

Grayson joined us first, and then Jax, both of them grabbing a couple slices of pizza before settling on the couch next to each other.

I staked out one of the oversized beanbags, and Lyn perched on the edge of a chair. A heavy silence settled over the room as we gave our attention to our food.

"You ready for RinCon?" Lyn asked Grayson.

Thank God for her and small talk. RinCon was an international gaming competition, put on by Rinslet, one of the largest gaming companies in the world, started by a couple of local guys.

Grayson flexed his fingers and rolled his wrists. "As ready as I'll ever be. I'm up against a newcomer from Korea this year, but I've got a good luck charm."

Grayson was an exhibition gamer. He used to compete. It was how he'd met Jax, who worked in sales with Chase at Rinslet. Grayson had been

looking for it

thinking about stepping back from the competitions anyway, but dating Jax made the decision easier. *Retiring* kept Grayson from traveling so much and helped them both avoid any conflict of interest. Now Grayson did most of his gaming online, and appeared at shows like this as part of the hype, to play against other top-tier gamers.

I glanced up to see Grayson watching me with an unreadable expression, and heat flooded my cheeks. "You'll do great," I mumbled through a mouthful of pizza.

"Your interview is tomorrow, isn't it?" Jax looked at me. "You excited?"

Tomorrow's meeting was the first of several I'd lined up, to speak with Hollywood costume designers and get myself on someone's team. The next step in my plan. I was nervous as fuck. "Of course. Opportunity of a lifetime, and all that." My reply came out with less enthusiasm than I intended.

Lyn's phone rang. She glanced at the screen and sighed so heavily, her body deflated. "I need to take this." As she answered, she left the room at a quick pace. Her voice faded then vanished.

Jax met my gaze. "You have the worst poker face in history. You said you were okay with this morning. Second thoughts?"

"I'm pretending it never happened, just like you asked." My retort came out with a sharper edge than

I intended. Where was the balance between discretion and embracing what we'd done? I'd had a total of two one-night stands in my life. Hookups with guys I met online, that ended with a walk of shame.

Grayson set aside his plate. "You're not pretending very well."

"And I could have sworn *you* called it *casual fun.* So what's with the silent treatment?" Jax said.

"I don't appreciate being treated like a dirty little secret." I winced at my immature retort. Neither of them was being aggressive. They seemed willing to talk through this, and I'd prefer to still be on speaking terms with them at the end of the day.

Jax scowled. "You think—"

"That's not what he meant." Grayson's tone was kinder than Jax's.

Calm down. Be a grown-up about this. "Explain it to me."

"Not if you're going to take it out of context." Jax sounded frustrated and… hurt?

"How else am I going to take you?"

"Tight and slick, just like earlier." He winked.

Heat flooded my cheeks. Effective way to shift the mood in the room. "One, that doesn't make any sense, and two, you said *we should keep this between us.* Not the sweetest thing to hear after sex."

"The *you're incredible* didn't stick?" Jax asked.

looking for it

Grayson crossed the room to sit on the floor next to my beanbag. The nearness wasn't unusual between us, but today it made me question so much.

"We asked for discretion because of Chase," he said.

Bros before hos? "I don't talk about my sex life with my brother."

"But we run in the same circles… obviously." Grayson settled his hand on my arm, searing my skin. "It's going to get back to him. And in the past, he's asked us—"

"His exact words were, *Keep your grubby dicks off my sister*," Jax said.

Not the nicest way for Chase to address his best friends, but he'd always been protective of me.

Wait. This meant he felt like he had a reason to make that request. Was that good or bad? I couldn't find a reply.

"The point was… *is*"—Grayson sighed—"we're not looking at you any differently—"

"I am." Jax smirked.

Grayson rolled his eyes, but a hint of a smile shone through. *Comforting.* "We're not looking at you with any less respect or any more assumption."

Jax's grin grew. "The lust hasn't decreased any, either."

He was lusting after me before? A tiny nag in the back of my mind repainted that moment in high school. He'd apologized. We'd moved on, or I wouldn't be talking to him now. None of those reassurances extinguished that spark of doubt. And here I was, not responding, while they tried to soothe my mind.

I needed to say something.

Grayson placed a finger under my chin and raised my gaze to his. "If you're not okay with what happened, say so now, and we can figure it out." He sounded so genuine.

My racing thoughts were slowing, and the nagging in my gut was fading at their insistence we use now to make things right. "I'm okay with it. Great with it. It was amazing." Was it okay to say that out loud? It should be.

"Something we agree on." Jax winked.

"...*I said no*." Lyn's shout echoed through the top floor of the building. "If you don't like my answer—even if you do—you can fuck all the way off." She stormed back into the room and threw her phone at her chair. It bounced once, and then settled. Red blotches marred her face, and she was shaking.

The conversation with Grayson and Jax took a backseat to Lyn's distress. It felt like we'd worked things out, anyway. I needed to adjust my perspective on how to act around them.

I extracted myself from my seat and approached Lyn, in case hugs were needed. "What happened?"

looking for it

She pinched the bridge of her nose and took a few deep breaths. "It was that asshole, who wants to buy the building. I want to blast out a warning to any woman considering dating him that he doesn't know how to take *no* for an answer. Fucking troglodyte."

"I can pound his face in for you," Jax offered.

Lyn let out a tiny laugh. "I'm good, thanks. But I'll keep the offer in mind." She looked at Grayson. "You're still coming over for Cosplay Christmas, aren't you?"

In other words, she wanted to change the subject. I respected that.

Grayson nodded. "Absolutely. I'm Sadie's to use and abuse, while the entire internet watches."

Hello, new fantasies. I needed to redraw the lines between the vivid images my brain liked to provide me with, and reality.

Chapter Five

I'd never been more nervous about a job interview in my life. Not that I'd had to deal with them since my channel took off a couple years ago and I started earning enough to pay the bills.

But today wasn't just about a job. It was about *the* job. The career I dreamed about. I looked myself over in the mirror one more time. The violet in my hair was vibrant, no roots showing. My makeup was on point. My outfit was the perfect way to present myself. It was a business suit, with subtle hints of evening gown worked into the trim and blouse. Professional but creative, to show off what I could do when I was given freedom.

I took several calming breaths and sat in front of my laptop. The call wasn't for another ten minutes, but I didn't know what else to do besides pace until I wore a path in the carpet. I'd posted several pictures of the outfit online, with a teaser that I hoped to share good news soon.

I fiddled with my phone, which I'd set to silent. There were three text messages. The first two were

looking for it

from Anne and Chase, wishing me luck. I'd read the third a ridiculous number of times. It was a good-luck message as well, but Jax sent it and Grayson chimed in. For someone who insisted one-time sex wouldn't change anything, I couldn't stop thinking it had changed everything.

Did I mind? All I knew was I couldn't hook up with them again. But damn, I wanted to.

Falling into that merry-go-round of thought would wait. It was almost time. I sat myself in front of my camera. The lighting and angle in my new room were perfect—I tested both with a couple of livestreams since yesterday. Any still-packed boxes were tucked away, and just enough of my room was visible to imply my personality without saying too much.

My stomach dropped into my shoes when my video-chat software rang. One more deep breath, then I answered.

The woman who appeared on my screen wasn't the one I expected. She introduced herself as *Kayla*, Ms. G's Assistant. Perhaps this was a few minutes of screening, or she'd keep me company until my Ms. G was available. A designer with her skill and reputation had to have a packed schedule.

I gave Kayla my warmest smile and let everything fall away except the person I was on camera. "It's so great to talk to you. I've really been looking forward to this conversation. You and Ms. G and the entire staff do such amazing work. The outfits in the newest fantasy adaptation were one-of-a-kind incredible." I stopped myself before I dove into fangirl gushing. I wanted them to know I was familiar with their designs, without talking so much they couldn't.

Kayla's smile brightened. "We're glad you reached out to us as well. It's always wonderful to connect with fresh talent. Your work is amazing. Not quite up to the standard we require from our designers, but you do have potential."

Mentally, I wavered. Feedback was good, especially from someone of this caliber. And they'd agreed to talk to me, so it wasn't all lip service. "I'm always willing to learn. Teach me and mold me."

"I'm happy to hear that." Did her voice just become a little more artificial, or was the mask over my wounded ego projecting? "Ms. G is so sorry she couldn't speak with you herself, but she'd like me to introduce you to a course we offer. It's an intimate, online setting. Rarely more than thirty people."

I— What? Maybe this was how they trained new hires? "Tell me more. Is this like some sort of remote internship?"

"In a way, yes. Your final design, the one you create for your grade, will be considered by Ms. G. If she feels you've done exceptional work, we

looking for it

consider offering you an internship. That will be local to L.A., and we provide a small stipend once you arrive."

None of this sounded like what I expected, or even legit. "And then you hire those interns?"

"If they work out, absolutely."

"I see. And this course is free?" Of course it was. She was about to laugh at me for even asking.

Kayla chuckled. "Ms. G's time is valuable. The course is five thousand dollars, but we do offer installment plans. If you're hired, the remainder of your balance is waived."

Anger flooded in, to mingle with my hurt and disbelief. "So basically, these interviews are your way of taking advantage of potential designers looking for an in."

"They're an excellent opportunity for people serious about their craft." Kayla's sunny mask cracked. "This is a chance to work with the best and get a foot up in an industry that touches every genre of film. Open slots in this program are rare, and you're fortunate to be offered one."

"Wow. I bet the internet would love to hear about this." Fuck pretenses and false smiles. This was some serious bullshit.

Kayla glowered. "You signed a non-disclosure agreement as part of this interview. I assure you, our lawyers do not take slander lightly. If you pass up this chance, if you leave a bad taste in our mouths, you will *never* work in Hollywood."

The idea of losing access to my dream curdled in my gut. She had to be making an empty threat. "I'll take that chance. Thank you for your time." I disconnected before she could reply.

I made sure all connections were closed, and resisted the urge to slam my laptop shut as I lowered the lid. Tears pricked the inside of my eyelids, as I sank back in my chair. Were they sadness? Fury? A heavy dose of both?

Was Kayla right, that I wasn't as good as I thought? Was that why I couldn't get anyone else to talk to me? Or was this one designer taking advantage of people? How many costumers had they taken advantage of? And what was it about me that said, *I'm so desperate, you can scam me out of five grand*?

I sat there, as minutes ticked away, letting my rage simmer into a thick, gooey mess in my thoughts. Ms. G wasn't getting away with this. I'd write a scathing email. Would I be the first? Would it be used against me when it came to other career opportunities? Did I care?

I opened my laptop again. A barking laugh choked from my throat when I saw an email waiting for me from Kayla. She was definitely getting a piece of my mind.

looking for it

The body of the message wasn't a nice, personalized little note. It looked more like a newsletter. It thanked me for my time and offered a link to more information about the course. And at the bottom of it all, it reminded me, *This email was sent from an unmonitored box. Do not reply.*

Fucking bitch. Curiosity and anger had me clicking the link. It took me to a pretty page with pictures of lots of smiling people near ornate costumes, and brief, content-less blurbs about how amazing this course was.

I was more interested in the *Terms and Conditions*. One lesson I was grateful I'd learned early on in my career—always know what people are doing with my intellectual property. This company was keeping it. Any designs submitted, proposed, or posted in the discussion room during the course were property of Ms. G.

Apparently, I could be more furious. I took screenshots of everything, and captured a PDF of the email as proof. I needed to call Anne and go downstairs to let Lyn know how things went. But I needed to type first, while the rage and thoughts were still fresh.

The world was going to know about this bullshit. I'd do a live feed. I'd link to evidence. As the list ticked off in my head, my fingers flew over the keyboard, composing a list of talking points for me to cover when I addressed my followers. In the next few hours, millions of people would know what was happening in one corner of Hollywood.

My anger didn't diminish as I re-read, revised, and relentlessly polished. A little voice I didn't care for joined the chorus, telling me this was a mistake. They'd threatened me.

It didn't matter. Ms. G was scamming people, and the world needed to know before they took advantage of anyone else.

A knock on my door made me jump. Shit, it was almost two. I'd been at this for hours. I was sufficiently collected to talk to Lyn. "Come in."

Jax poked his head into my room. Lust bounded in and muddled my fury at the softness around his eyes.

"Are you all right?" he asked.

"No, I'm not. What are you doing here?" I made sure to ask calmly. I wasn't angry at him.

He stepped inside and mostly closed the door behind him. Jax dressed for work was as delicious as Jax in jeans and a T-shirt. He embodied everything about the phrase *Suit Porn*. "We all got worried when you didn't message anyone back. I had a client lunch down the street, and it gave me an excuse to check on you. Did they tell you that you have to wait to start? Or are they making you pack up and leave us right away?"

looking for it

My brain stalled. He was assuming I got the job. There was no doubt in his questions, only concern.

"I didn't get it," I said.

"What? But you're the best."

"Not according to them." I couldn't hold back any longer. I'd spent hours writing out my thoughts, and now I had an audience. I let the story spill out.

His expression shifted from sympathetic to one of an anger that matched my own. "Are you fucking kidding me? Who do I need to crucify?"

"I'm going to tell the entire internet." I was encouraged by his response. "You can give me a signal boost."

Jax frowned. "Don't do that."

There it was—the lack of support I'd feared. Any hope that had blossomed since he showed up wilted and withered and exploded in a cloud of disappointed dust.

Chapter Six

I stared at Jax with disbelief. "Did you hear me?" He'd looked sympathetic. "They're ripping people off. Not just me. They didn't manufacture a several-thousand-dollar course specifically for me."

"And you signed an NDA."

Fucking logic. "If they come after me, at least I've warned others. I'll fight back." Could I? How badly would they ruin me? Damn him, for zeroing in on the one point that had me wavering.

"It's not that easy, and it's not going to be cheap. Even an initial push back, beyond yielding to their demands, will make their five thousand look like pocket change." He sounded kind.

I didn't want that. I wanted him to be sneering, all-but implying I was being stupid, so I could keep raging and suck him into the bubble of what irritated me. "Since when do you know so much about these things?"

He raised an eyebrow and pursed his lips.

Ah. Not a dumb question unless one knew who he worked for. Rinslet had built a large part of their

looking for it

reputation on not fitting in. They were strategic about who they pissed off, and they knew how to spin almost any bad press. As part of their sales department, Jax had to be familiar with all of their talking points. Chase had gone on about it at length and with great fascination when he was in training.

But— "I can't let this go. They're taking advantage of people. This isn't just about me."

"I'm not saying *walk away*. Be smart about how you retaliate."

"How?"

"Let me talk to a friend in Legal. Save your rant until I have answers, and once you're protected, we can tear them down."

"*We?*" I liked the warm glow that spread inside with his support and offer of help.

He flashed me one of those sexy smirks that sent my imagination running rampant. "You roped me in when you gave me deets. Now you're stuck with me until things are resolved."

"I won't complain about that." Damn him for making me almost smile in the midst of my rage.

Jax reached for the door. "Text Anne and Chase and tell them you're all right. Chase wants to take you out to celebrate. Tell him you're up for commiseration instead, and he's buying the drinks."

"Bossy much?"

"You know you love it." He winked and was gone.

My feelings about the not-interview hadn't changed, but I was doing better, thanks to Jax's surprise visit.

He was eye candy and taken by an amazing man. Fantasy material, not swoon-after and crush-on material. I had to remember that.

I also had to go online and tell my followers my big news had been postponed, and thank them for the good wishes. My heart sank again. Talk about a soul-crushing reality check.

Lyn invited everyone to hold my commiseration party in her basement. The space had originally been built out as an over-sized den, complete with a pool table, bar, and kitchenette. I insisted she didn't need to cook for us. She countered she had new appetizer recipes and needed a test audience.

It was hard to argue against her cooking. Besides, if we drank here, no one had to be the designated driver. The basement had plenty of couches for everyone.

Chase brought Asahi beer, because he was a beer snob.

looking for it

Anne brought Guinness because, *Chase brought that pale-ass lager, didn't he?* I'd known her most of my life. When we were kids, we'd tell people we were twins, both of us the same height and build, with dark-blond hair. Her hair was a shorter pixie cut now, and its natural color. We were about five-six and could share clothes, but she was more comfortable in jeans and baggy T-shirts, where I preferred things more form-fitting. And she was still as much my sister as anyone ever would be.

Jax and Grayson brought champagne and flowers. There was no explanation, but daises were my favorite, and I couldn't hide my grin when Grayson handed them to me.

Everyone offered hugs and sympathy. It killed me to keep my mouth shut. To not tell them, *Turns out it was a massive fucking scam.* I hated keeping secrets, and my job-interview news plus my *it's just casual fun* hook up with Jax and Grayson were bursting to get out.

I needed more of a distraction than rounds of pity and commiseration. "We should play something," I announced. It was almost a given that we'd split into teams of boys versus girls. We were evenly matched at all of our favorites, though some of us were better at each than the rest of us. Pool. Dance Dance Revolution.

"Darts," Grayson said.

Chase handed Grayson and me each a beer. "Neither of you is drunk enough for darts."

I turned wide, sad eyes toward Chase and batted my eyelashes. "But I'm so wounded and heartbroken." I managed the perfect balance of teasing and pathetic in my voice.

"Fine." Chase let out an exaggerated huff. "I suppose you've earned the right to throw sharp, pointy things at a target. But no one's going easy on you."

My grin was back. "Like that's a concern."

We didn't play with traditional rules. The team with the most points at the end of one round won. We did have an extra set of rules we tacked on to anything we played as a group. Trying to distract the other team was both allowed and encouraged, as long as there was no touching, no stepping in someone's line of sight, and no jump scares. The distractions were frequently more fun and competitive than the game itself.

When we were younger, it was Chase and Jax versus Anne and me. We stopped for a while after I met Lyn, because the teams were uneven. But once Grayson and Jax started dating, it was *game on*. It helped that Grayson was the only one of them who could match me at darts.

Anne was up first, with Lyn and me cheering her loudly.

looking for it

Anne lined up her first throw.

"Shame we're not playing DDR." Chase's tone was deceptively casual. What was he up to? "You're always nice to watch on the dance pads."

Anne threw. She fell far right of center, but it was a steady toss. "You just hate that you suck at this as badly as I do." She readied her second dart.

"If we're having a sucking contest, I want different rules. The *no touching* has to go. A little privacy might be nice."

"I don't need to hear that." I exaggerated my protest. His teasing seemed to get to me more than Anne. Her next throw hit the board, and her third landed in the wall.

Pretty much what I expected. But she made me look like spastic rag doll in DDR, and I didn't have a problem admitting it.

Chase went next. With a glance from Anne, I knew what she was up to. We gave him silence for his first two throws, while the guys chanted his name.

He lined up his last shot.

Anne let out a sharp wolf whistle. "Wow. Did you see her?"

Chase whipped his head in her direction, and everyone laughed.

"No one here but us, bro." Jax slapped him on the back.

Chase fixed his gaze on Anne. "Thought maybe you saw your reflection."

"Right." She raised her eyebrows and pursed her lips.

Jax stepped up to the line next, all swagger and confidence.

"Cocky for a man who's about to lose," Anne teased.

He kept his attention focused on the dartboard.

Lyn had her phone out. She swiped the screen, and a cash register sound echoed from the speakers.

Jax didn't flinch. He also barely hit the board.

She cycled through several more sounds in rapid succession. Cheers. Boos. A rooster crowing.

Jax made his second shot.

A drawn-out gasp, like someone on the edge of ecstasy, echoed from Lyn's phone.

Oh God. That was me.

Jax's last dart landed flat side against the wall and tumbled to the ground.

She must have taken that from one of my videos when I was messing around. I shot Lyn a glare, and she shrugged.

"Fair's fair," she said, and grabbed three darts to take her turn.

Lyn and Grayson were impossible to ruffle. Neither of them flinched or faltered, regardless of what we said. And Grayson hit every shot

looking for it

beautifully, with two in the bullseye and one in the treble ring.

Which meant I had to be spot on my game. I should have made Grayson go last, to see if any pressure got to him. But as a competition gamer, he'd learned how to let most of that stress roll off him.

I took my place in front of the board, darts in hand. Grayson stepped up behind me. He didn't break the *no touching* rule, but he was so close I felt his heat.

"I want to watch how a real master works," he said. "See this from the same angle you do." He wasn't so near that his breath brushed my skin, but I swore I felt his words rolling over me.

Whatever he was doing, it wouldn't work. I grabbed my focus and landed my first throw in the treble ring.

"You ever have trouble with the tip not sticking in?" Grayson asked.

A laugh bubbled up inside at the innuendo. If I gave in to amusement, I wouldn't be able to recover. "No."

"Any problems with it going in too deep?" Everyone was silent except Grayson.

I threw again and hit the bullseye. "No."

"Hmm…" Grayson dragged out the sound. "So it never gets stuck because it's a tight fit?"

This was killing me. I was so close to done, though. If I could hit the treble ring again, we'd win. "Nope. Never been an issue."

"Never?"

"Not even once." I aimed.

"What about when the tip gets jerked up at the wrong angle, and you don't expect it, and you get jizz in your hair?" Jax asked.

Laughter and disbelief tore from me, and I completely missed my mark. It took me several seconds to collect myself and shoot a glare at him, but with his smug expression staring back, I couldn't hold onto my composure. "That was anything but subtle." I finally managed. "There was *zero* innuendo there."

"Innuendo isn't against the rules. And she started it." He nodded toward Lyn.

She smirked. "Don't know what you're talking about."

With the game over, we fell into other conversations. The night sped by quickly, the way it tended to when we were all together. A few hours later, I found myself in the upstairs kitchen, looking for juice or something else to drink that wasn't alcohol.

"So, what's up with you three?" Anne's soft question startled me.

looking for it

I hadn't talked to her since *the event*—had it only been a day?—and it wasn't the kind of thing I wanted to share over text. I could imagine the message now. *Guess who I had sex with?*

I could also imagine what she'd say next. That was the other thing holding me back. She was there when Jax hurt me, so long ago. She helped me pick up the pieces. Anne was the one person most likely to remind me this was a mistake.

"What do you mean?" I winced even before I finished asking the question. I didn't want to lie to her.

She crossed the room, to steal a sip of my Coke. "I *mean* they're flirting with you. Okay, so Grayson always does—"

He did?

"—but I swear I heard Jax get an erection when Lyn played that sound clip of you."

"So... yeah, something happened. But it was a one-time thing, and we're all being discreet."

"*All*? As in—"

"All three of us." If my confession to Lyn was any indication, it was best to get some of the details out there up front.

Anne stared at me, mouth slightly agape. Here it came. "No shit. How was it?"

Not the first thing I expected her to say, but it was the perfect response. "Amazing. And I'm dying, not being able to tell anyone."

"Lyn knows."

"Lyn guessed. It happened yesterday. It made us late to her house, and she put some pieces together."

Anne leaned against the counter next to me, her arm pressed against mine. "But it was only a one-time thing, right?" The awe and surprise faded from her voice.

"I already said it was."

"Because if Jax hurts you again, I'll make him suffer," Anne said.

There it was. "He's not going to. It's not that kind of thing." Except the nagging part of my mind that agreed with her on the possibility was begging me to listen to it. To her.

"Okay." Anne let out a long breath. "Both of them. Really? Do I get details?"

"When we're not surrounded by prying ears, yes. Like I said, it was amazing." I really was dying to talk about it. But my nagging voice didn't shut up because Anne had moved past her concerns.

Chapter Seven

Between sitting on my plans to expose Ms. G, and trying not to overthink Grayson and Jax's behavior post move-in, I had a lot of excess energy to burn. I poured a bit of it into decorating my room for Christmas. Evergreen-colored garland decorated with strings of red and white lights hung along my wall, and I had holiday wall scrolls to break up the design. I loved the way it looked for me and on camera.

That was done now, and I could go back to focusing on acting normal around Grayson. That should be easy, since he and I did things together all the time similar to what I had planned for today.

I dropped into my computer chair, careful not to let my outfit ride too high or drop too low, and surveyed the filming corner of my bedroom. In a few minutes, I was taking the last clips I needed to create my *Furry Christmas Cosplay How-To* video.

The outfits themselves were easy to make, and I'd filmed myself doing so. The red fleece tops were trimmed with white and had hoods with puppy ears for the guys and kitty ears for the girls. My outfit had a skirt that barely covered my ass, and thigh-high stockings. There were two variations on each top. A long-sleeved, jacket style, and a sleeveless fitted vest.

Grayson was going to be my model for the puppy clothing, one piece at a time, to show them off, and then the entire outfit. He'd done this for me so often, I knew his measurements by heart, and the vest would give my subscribers the fan service they expected from him.

They'd get the same from me. I was wearing the skirt and the low-cut top that pushed my cleavage up. I was going to look incredible, helping him dress up.

There were two big upsides to these collaborations—they brought in both of our fan bases and pushed my viewer numbers through the roof, but more importantly, it gave me the perfect excuse to run my hands all over Grayson's body.

Which... How did I ever think that was innocent? Because he had a boyfriend? He'd watched—jerked off—while said boyfriend fucked me. A pulse throbbed between my thighs at the whispers of memory. Even if the touching *didn't* mean anything, I'd never believe it again.

A sharp whistle cut through my swelling desire, and I whirled to see Grayson in my doorway. It was instinct to strike a sexy pose—our joint videos

looking for it

frequently started with his appreciation for my outfit of the day—but today his reaction also cranked the heat racing through my veins. How long until my face matched my clothes?

The way he leaned against my doorframe accentuated the ripple of muscle along his torso and upper arms. "Where do you want me, bosslady?"

On the bed. On the floor. Pinning me against the wall… "It's a standard shoot." I jerked a thumb toward an empty space I'd set up for this part of recording. "A piece of clothing at a time, and pose."

"All right." He kicked away from the wall. His cheerful tone clashed with his frown.

"What's wrong?"

"When do we film me helping you into and out of your clothes?"

That was new, even for us. I'm pretty sure I wouldn't have brushed off something that direct as status quo, in the past. "I'm not taking it off the table."

His grin turned my insides gooey.

Act normal. That was all I had to do.

Had we ever really been *normal*?

"Shirt off." I had a remote for my camera tucked under my bra strap. It would make it easier to keep both of us in the right position without having to record *everything*.

"I love the way you say that." Grayson, stripping his T-shirt off was a gorgeous sight to behold.

I took advantage of the half second his eyes were covered, to stare, when I should have been using the time to compose myself. Something about this situation had to change, or we wouldn't get any work done.

"You ready for RinCon?" I asked as I handed him the tail belt and stepped out of the frame.

He raised his brows but fitted the belt into place without argument.

I should have picked a better question to change the subject with. Not because it was unusual for us to talk about it—exactly the opposite. Our circle of friends lived and breathed RinCon in the weeks leading up to it, and there wasn't much left to say at this point. He was going to use this video as a teaser, to draw in more interest to his livestreams during the event.

But the con was all business to me. It was kind of like thinking about baseball, to ignore horniness. It wasn't working.

"Specifically, do you have any details you can share that no one else has?" I grabbed his vest off its mannequin. This part needed to be hands on. It was always more effective this way. I set the camera to record again and slid the fleece up his arms. Made a

looking for it

generous show of smoothing everything out as I glided my palms over his chest. Kept his tattooed arm pointed toward the camera.

Failed to ignore the prickles of desire racing over my skin and tightening in my nipples. Good thing this was a padded bra.

I finished my part and stepped back, to let him pose for the camera alone. Hood down, and then up. I paused the recording.

"They tell me there's a surprise coming, but no details," he said.

Something none of us had heard yet? "You're not just holding out on me to be clever?" I teased.

He shrugged out of the vest and held it out for me. When I stepped in to take it, he tweaked one of my kitty ears. "You look so adorable in these, I'd tell you the secrets of the universe if I knew them."

My heated cheeks were back. I turned away to hang up the top and hoped it would give my face time to pale again.

He grabbed my wrist, startling me, and turned me to face him. "We need to talk about the other day." His tone was serious, but a spark of playfulness danced behind his eyes.

"What about it? We're good. We all agreed." I was being awkward, but that would pass with time.

"We did. But I can't move past the jealousy."

Oh. My heart sank. I never wanted to be a wedge in their relationship. "I thought you were okay with it. I'm sorry. I didn't—"

He pressed a finger to my lips. "Don't apologize. Let me finish. I thought I was okay with it too—and don't misunderstand, watching you with Jax was good—but there's this little slice of envy that he got to feel you and I didn't."

And now my heart was not only fine, but also skipping. "I wouldn't want to leave you out."

"Me neither. Go figure." Grayson tugged me closer, dipped his head, and trailed his nose up the side of my neck.

Want clashed with concern. When I was with Jax, Grayson was there to give his explicit *okay*. This was different. "I don't want to come between you."

"He's okay with wherever this goes. In fact, I'm planning to tell him *everything* about what happens between us."

"Like what?" My question came out timid and breathy. I had my own fantasies, but I'd never dare say them out loud.

"Hmm..." Grayson settled his hands on my hips, on the bare skin above my skirt. "I'll tell him if your nipples taste like sugar. If your pussy is peach-flavored. How incredible you feel when I'm buried inside you. So if you have issues with me kissing and telling, say so."

looking for it

The only issue I had was that we weren't doing any of that yet. "Does that mean—" The question stuck in my throat.

"Does it mean what?"

"That he'll get off to the story of us together?" I barely heard myself ask the question, over the hammering of my pulse in my ears.

Grayson pressed his body into mine, heat searing through my thin outfit. "We both will." His voice was a low hum, licking temptation along my skin. "I'll be at his feet, sucking his cock, stroking my own during every delicious moment of the relived memory."

"Hot." I hadn't meant to say that aloud.

He scrapped his teeth along my neck and yanked down my hood. "My point exactly. Is that a *yes?*"

Was it? How many one-night stands did it take, before we passed some invisible line of *too many*? Everything had already changed. How much further was I willing to alter the relationship between the three of us?

Chapter Eight

I didn't need to think long about Grayson's offer. Longer than I did for most things, but he was too tempting to pass up. "That's a *yes*."

"Looks like I get to help you out of your costume, after all." Grayson grasped the hidden zipper on my top and tugged it down one agonizing tooth at a time, his gaze lingering on my breasts. "Every time you run your palms over my bare chest, I want to return the favor."

Seriously, how had I never noticed before that what we did was more than friendly? "Now's your chance."

"And what a chance it is." He glided his hands up my chest, to cup my breasts.

When he dragged his thumbs over my nipples, I felt the *zing* even though the padding of my bra. It was a sharp spark that raced along my every nerve ending.

Grayson pushed my top off my shoulders and tossed it aside. My bra came off next, leaving me

looking for it

exposed and topless. Every time he looked me over, a fresh wave of flames raced over me.

When his palms touched my bare skin, the heat intensified. He teased my pale pink swollen nubs. "Not just sugar. Bubblegum. Yum." He dipped his head to flick his tongue over one nipple, before drawing it into his mouth. He sucked and nibbled one side, while kneading the other.

Pleasure sped over me, and I pressed into his mouth. He switched to the other breast when I started to squirm. The longer he sucked, the damper my panties got. I wanted to reach between my legs and relieve the building anticipation.

Grayson grasped my wrist and moved my hand to his erection. I'd gotten a hint of how big he was the other day, but stroking him drove the point home. I traced the outline through denim, and his groan hummed across my skin. We were hooked in a delicious loop of pleasure.

He drifted his kisses lower, moving down my stomach and pulling away from my touch as he knelt in front of me. He shoved my skirt up and over my hips—another reason to love fleece—and scraped his teeth over my panties. "You're already wet."

Massive understatement. My laugh was breathy and strained, and most of my brain power was focused on my arousal. "*Already*? I'm surprised all that sucking and biting didn't make me come."

"No?" The way he looked up at me with that dark, open gaze, I felt like I was being worshiped. "Time to try something else." He looped his fingers in my panties and slid them down my legs. When he licked once along my damp lower lips, I moaned.

Could they hear me downstairs? Did I care?

Grayson stood, to lift me onto a nearby stool. As he knelt again, he spread my legs. His soft kisses started at my knee and traveled up my inner thigh.

Each brush of his lips against my skin cranked my anticipation higher, and I gripped the edge of the stool tightly. When he reached my core, I shivered and gasped in delight. He wrapped his lips around my clit to, suck and tease. I swear to God he was writing the alphabet with his tongue.

He slipped two fingers inside me, and hooked up, hitting the right spot and stealing my thoughts.

My breath came in short gasps, and I lost track of my own moans and whimpers. My head was light. He pushed me to the edge of climax and let me linger on that fine point.

I knotted my fingers in his hair. I didn't want to miss anything, and from the way his tongue was working frantically, neither did he.

Orgasm crashed over me in wave, tearing a scream from my throat. I ground into Grayson's face as I came, losing myself in the intense colors of

looking for it

pleasure that sparked in my thoughts and made my legs weak.

He pulled away as I loosened my grip, and sucked his fingers clean as he stood. "Definitely cherries and bubblegum. My new favorite flavors. Want a taste?" He pressed his mouth to mine, open and hungry.

Our first real kiss.

What an odd thought. I brushed it aside and dove into the feeling of him devouring my lips. The taste of myself. The way he kneaded my breast and swallowed my moans.

I wrapped my legs around his ass and pulled him in closer, until I could reach his belt.

He broke the kiss, to laugh against my lips. "Eager?"

"Aren't you?" I let desperation and need drive me as I undid his jeans. When I brushed his shaft, his throaty groan drilled into me. "Promises were made."

"They definitely were." Grayson reached into his back pocket while I worked him free. He rolled on a condom and pressed, to glide the head of his cock along the same path his tongue had followed.

I arched into the contact. He slid inside me, stretching me out and hitting deep. I needed to be a part of him. To feel as much as possible. I tightened my legs, to set a fast and frantic pace.

He gripped my hips tight, slowing me down. With each thrust, he withdrew almost to the tip before plunging back into me again. My opening clenched at the delicious repeated sensation of penetration.

Grayson slanted his mouth over mine, to kiss me hard, and increased the pace at the same time. As he slammed against me, he struck that perfect spot inside, nudging me toward another orgasm.

The build-up pushed me right to that point between pleasure and discomfort. He nipped my bottom lip and pinched a nipple, rolling the nub between his fingers. The extra sensations knocked me into climax. I clenched around him, milking him and keeping him buried inside me until it was too much and not enough at the same time.

His grunts told me he was close. His pounding hit frantic, before jarring to a shuddering pause, and then slowing again. He'd come too.

The desperation faded as he stopped, but the warm fuzzies flitting through me lingered.

Grayson rested his forehead on my shoulder while we both fought to catch our breath. My legs were too wobbly to stay wrapped around him, but I hooked my fingers in the waistband of his jeans, holding him close and feeling as much of his skin as possible.

"You paused the camera?" he asked softly.

looking for it

"Yes."

"Shame. I'd have loved a souvenir of that. Then again, one with just you, legs spread and pussy exposed, giving us a private show…"

I liked every bit of that, except the *us*. That was what he and Jax were, though. An *us*. I wasn't a part of that, no matter how much I enjoyed these interludes. A stone settled in my heart. They had each other, and I was an intermission, like every other hookup they had. Was I okay with that?

Chapter Nine

Knowing people in the gaming industry had its perks. Today, it was backstage access to Grayson's opening day exhibition match. The audience would have a better view of his game, thanks to the giant screens that sat at the front of the room, but I had more fun watching him.

Being back here also gave me a much-needed respite from the crowds for a little bit and let me catch my breath. I could still hear them, but they weren't pressing in on me.

The last couple of days, I'd been too busy to put much thought into what happened with Grayson. I edited the video—which was a massive hit and led to dozens of extra pic requests today—and spent the rest of my time making sure my costumes and schedule were set for the con.

Everyone else had been as busy as me, but the couple of texts I got from Grayson lifted most of the lingering doubt I had about that incredible frozen moment. The texts were nothing overt, which was perfect; they let me know everything was all right.

looking for it

This morning's said, *See you at the match in a few hours x.*

Someone pressed into me from behind, and a faint but familiar whiff of cologne reached me. *Jax.* He was warm against my bare lower back, thanks to the exposed midriff on my costume de jour.

He brushed his lips along the outside of my ear, sending shivers over my skin. Though the assumption of his closeness wasn't new, I was enjoying it far more than I'd ever dared in the past.

"Grayson told me what you did." His whisper made his tone hard to decipher.

"He promised he would." And what a vivid, seductive promise it had been. Did Grayson use similar words telling Jax?

Jax nipped my earlobe, and a jolt raced through my veins. "The plan is to get you addicted to us, so you can't help but come back for more," he said.

The emcee started working the crowd, and cheers exploded around us. My focus was elsewhere. I leaned some of my weight against Jax. The magic in the air here added to the floating giddiness in my head. "I thought this was just casual fun," I teased.

"Your words. Though it *is* fun." He glided his hands down my exposed sides, to rest on my hips right above the waistband of my low-rise jeans. "If I feel you up right here, does it take us a step closer to being more than *casual*?"

Did he want that? He wasn't exactly being subtle.

What about his relationship? What about the past? The questions slammed into my thoughts with a quiet cruelty, bringing images with them of a decade ago—a piece of my life I'd forgiven him for. So of course the reminder chose now to gnaw at me.

That didn't mean I wanted to push him away. "It takes us a step closer to getting caught." I kept my tone light and playful.

"Tempting, isn't it?"

It was. Much more than it should be. A rush of desire pulsed under my skin, similar to what I felt when Grayson watched me with Jax, but this was peppered with a hotter blend of spice. I wasn't quite bold enough to fool around with nothing but a curtain between us and an audience of several hundred, but it could be fun… "We'll miss the match."

"He'll win. He always does."

Another reason Grayson was an exhibition player now instead of a competitor.

"But never if you're uncertain." Jax's hands fell away. He didn't step back, though. "I talked to a friend about your situation."

I didn't realize I hadn't expected him to follow through until he said he did. The way he changed the subject jarred me, and the topic dragged my stress back. "What did they say?"

looking for it

"I have a letter for you to send Ms. G's office. It tells them you consider the NDA null and void because you signed on the promise of a job interview, and it's obvious they never had any intentions of interviewing you. Along with the letter, you reiterate that you're going to make their information public, and then you publish what you have."

It was too easy. I shouldn't complain. "Just like that."

"That's what I'm told."

"That won't stop them from coming after me."

Jax sighed. "No. They can—and probably will—still pursue. But other people will come forward when they see that you have. Especially if the reason you speak up is are part of your exposé."

"And if others have similar stories, it corroborates mine." I hated that my word about the situation wasn't sufficient, but one person claiming, *I was scammed by Hollywood*, would fade into the background. Numbers gave me credibility.

"I think, if you keep pushing any correspondence they send you while this moves forward…"

"The internet will bully them back." Large chunks of this situation were unfolding before my eyes.

"Basically."

Wow. "Normally I'm opposed to the dogpile mentality."

Jax rested his hands on my hips again. "What if it's more of a puppy pile? All three of us, collapsing in a tangled heap of exhaustion and limbs after some incredible sex?"

All of us... The longer he talked, the more I wanted to take him up on that *feel me up right here* offer. "You're horrible."

"You said I was good."

"You were incredible."

He rested his head against mine. "That does sound like me. When are you going live with this?"

Our not even thinly veiled conversation about me sleeping with him and his boyfriend? That was for us alone. But he was talking about Ms. G. "This afternoon, if I can. That gives me the extra viewership of everyone tuned in for RinCon." And plenty of time to stress, as I waited for the fallout.

"Do it. We'll take you out after, to keep you distracted."

I kind of loved how he was in my head. "I'm not going to be a lot of fun if I can't stop thinking about it." Not just the blowback from Ms. G, but the hate this would earn me because I dared speak up about *anything*.

"We can be *very* distracting."

looking for it

I adored his confidence. The attention. How much he was doing on my behalf. "You've set my expectations high."

"Where they deserve to be," Jax said.

If only I could give all my attention to him and Grayson, and ignore the holes worry was trying to tear in my soul.

Chapter Ten

Mid-afternoon, I called it a day from RinCon and headed home. My *Expose Ms. G* post was written up, but I had to add my letter to her, then re-read it. Again. And then again. Before I recorded my video.

When that was done, I checked it over and over, the need for perfection warring with my desire to act now. It was time to hit *Post*.

My phone chimed with a new text from Grayson.

Where are you?

Home. Contemplating the fate of my career, I replied.

Knock knock. His text coincided with a knock on my bedroom door, making my heart leap into my throat.

Thank God for a distraction. "Why'd you ask if you knew?" I said as I swung the door open.

"Sorry, what?" Grayson's gaze drifted up my body, Jax's doing the same.

Maybe I should have gotten dressed after my shower. At least I was wearing a robe, and I didn't

looking for it

mind at all the way they were looking at me. "You wouldn't have made the trip if you weren't pretty sure I was here."

Grayson looked up first, an easy smile sliding into place. "It was more fun this way. Chase said Anne said you took off, so..."

"They didn't mention *what* you took off. Probably for the best." Jax was still staring at my chest.

I snapped my fingers in front of his face, finally drawing his attention. "Am I late?"

"We're early," Jax said. "Something told me you were sitting here, conflicted over whether or not your posts were perfect, so you're going to pull the trigger, hand him your phone to keep you from checking it, and get dressed so we can go mingle in the courtesy suites."

"Just like that?" I shouldn't protest—I desperately needed the distraction Jax had promised.

Grayson held out his hand. "Just like that."

I handed over my phone. Two seconds later, my post was live on the internet and my heart rate had doubled.

Wait. They said courtesy suites? "If you're talking to clients and vendors, I'm not going to be a great conversationalist."

"You'll be too stunningly gorgeous for anyone to notice." Jax assured me.

I raised my brows. "You only want me as an accessory?"

"I want you for so much more, but no. I'd never relegate you to something like *accessory*. That's what this pretty boy is for." Jax jerked his head toward Grayson.

Grayson chuckled. "Such an asshole. You're lucky I love you." He brushed his lips over Jax's.

It didn't matter that the kiss was quick and something I'd seen over and over. Tonight, the sight sent tingles prickling along my skin. It was sweet and hot at the same time. How had I never noticed before how sexy that was? Easy adoration flowed between them. What they had was so real. So tangible. So very much what I wanted to find with my perfect guy.

"Get dressed. We'll wait downstairs," Jax said.

Boldness rushed into my veins, buoyed by an excess of adrenaline that wanted me to run away from what I just put out into the world. "You're not going to help?" I looked up at Grayson through my eyelashes. "Pretty sure there was talk of you dressing me."

Jax sucked in a hard breath.

Grayson bit his bottom lip. "Pretty sure we already did that. Still, a repeat is tempting. But we'd be so late if we did to you now even a fraction of the things we want to."

looking for it

"All right." I managed a pout despite the way his words made my nipples tighten and my thighs squeeze together.

As I dressed, I understood exactly what Grayson meant about certain activities making us late. The brief teasing alone tempted me to pull out my vibrator. Or even better, yank the guys back up here.

Instead, I smoothed my favorite little black dress into place—the one with the scoop neck, fitted body, and long skirt with the slits that ran most of the way up my thighs. It was a stretchy fabric that looked like satin that shimmered but allowed me to move freely. I'd done my hair and makeup for the video, so there was only a little touch-up there, and I was ready.

I twitched, to reach for my phone. To take *a quick glance* at my messages. Thank God for Grayson, confiscating the device.

When I descended the back stairs to where the guys and Lyn were chatting in the kitchen, I was greeted with a trio of whistles. I looked amazing, but the confirmation did great things for my ego.

Grayson grasped my fingers before I reached the bottom steps, and I felt like I was making a grand entrance at a ball.

Kind of like that New Year's dance would have been, so many years ago.

The thought slipped into my head without permission, carried on a cloud of doubt and history, and I shoved it aside.

We headed out to Grayson's truck. It was a snug fit, but since he had a bench seat, it would be far more comfortable than Jax's BMW Z4. Being pressed between them, with the weight of strong arms and thighs resting against mine, was a much better distraction from what I'd done than their random banter about who they met and what they talked about at the show today.

What should have been a five- or ten-minute drive turned into nearly thirty, thanks to holiday traffic downtown. Not that I minded. I was warm and safe.

We pulled into the line for valet parking at the hotel where the parties were taking place.

Grayson rested a hand on my upper thigh. "I changed my mind." His comment was casual. The way he teased the slit of my dress with his thumb was almost possessive.

My pulse hammered in my ears, as if my heart knew something my head hadn't figured out yet. "About what?"

"Helping you with your clothes. Take off your panties."

"Here?" I squeaked. We sat higher than most everyone else, and it was dark in the cab, but we were

looking for it

still crawling slower than foot traffic, and surrounded by people. So why did the command spread through me on a rush of desire?

Jax slipped his hand under my skirt, to brush my bare skin. He trailed his fingers up the inside of my leg. "Unless you want to wait until we're closer."

I could tell them *no*, but my heart slammed against my ribs with the need to see where this went. I tried to be discreet about lifting my butt off the seat, and both of their touches fell away. It took inching the slits of my dress up over my hips to grasp the elastic of my panties and slide them down my legs. Stretchy-sparkly dress for the win.

I slipped the underwear off my legs. The instant I straightened in my seat again, Grayson tugged the lacy clothing from my hands and shoved it in his pocket.

"For safe keeping." The gruffness in his voice was like desire gliding over me.

And then Jax's hand was back under my dress, as he teased his fingers along my bare mound. Could anyone see? Did I care? His touch was light and playful, slipping easily along my skin and between my folds.

I half-closed my eyes, falling into the sensation, as he glided closer to my opening.

When his touch fell away, my eyes flew open. We were at the valet station, and Jax was sucking on his fingers.

A groan bubbled inside, and I swallowed it. *Fuck me.* No, really. Here. Now. I didn't care who saw.

Jax helped me from the truck as though nothing out of the ordinary had happened.

Grayson joined us. "You didn't save any for me."

Jax stuck two fingers in Grayson's mouth. This time a whimper did escape my throat, earning me a pair of satisfied smirks. Would my magical dress hide any wet spots? Because it would need to if this kept up.

We headed inside. Limitless lights and trees and ornaments greeted us, brightening the hotel and the various conference rooms on the mail floor. RinCon during the day was for the fans and press—the big games rolled out, the demos happened. At night, in the multitude of vendor-sponsored rooms with open bars and buffets, the business deals were churned out.

People were just starting to trickle in, but Jax and everyone in sales would be here to mingle and eavesdrop and spread goodwill.

And I was wandering through these crowds of businesspeople with no panties on. It was insane, and

looking for it

I was so turned on, I wasn't sure I could talk without bursting into giggles if anyone addressed me.

"Hey, guys." Chase's voice cut through every layer of haze in my head.

Talk about an arousal killer. I turned to face him, and gave him a smile.

"You here for work?" he asked me.

"Exactly the opposite." I was going to give him as close to the truth as I could without saying, *Do you have any idea how fuckably hot your friends are?* "I'm stressed about my latest video, so they're distracting me."

He furrowed his brow, and I could almost hear the gears turning in his head. "Something's different between the two of you." He was talking about me and Jax.

"Help a woman move her mattress, and the dynamic changes. That's just the way things work." Jax's reply was smooth and without hesitation.

I was grateful we'd agreed to discretion. I'd have to apologize later for the fit I threw about their original request.

"Uh-huh," Chase said flatly.

Grayson tangled his fingers with Jax's. "Pretty sure you're imagining things."

"Hughes." Someone called Chase from across the room.

He glanced at us one more time, shook his head, and trotted off to catch up with the guy who summoned him.

"Just so you know, that wasn't because you're a dirty secret." Jax moved his free hand to the small of my back, his voice so low only we would hear. "All three of us need to be on the same page when we tell people."

Tell people. His statement added a reality filter to an erotically surreal situation, and my thoughts revolted. "What is there to tell?"

"Part of what we'll discuss when we're not in the middle of a crowd of software-company execs," Grayson said.

I didn't have an argument. What *were* we doing? I reached for Grayson's sleeve, to tug them aside and ask. Despite what he said, now was as good a time as any to talk.

"Grayson." A woman approached, putting a dent in my plan. "I was hoping you'd be here."

"Lee. Great to meet you face-to-face." Grayson shook her hand. "This is Sadie, and my boyfriend, Jax."

An ache pinged in my chest at the introduction. But it was a solid reminder, and one I needed—they were *them*, and I wasn't a part of that.

Chapter Eleven

I gave Lee a warm smile. "How do you and Grayson know each other?"

"Lee's my contact for the VR hardware I've been streaming with," Grayson said. He had early access to some top-of-the-line gear that was lighter weight and higher powered than anything on the market.

From what I'd seen and what he'd said, even with the bugs in the beta version, it blew everything else out of the water. "It's amazing tech," I said.

"I've got to know." Lee dropped her voice to a stage whisper. "Have you hacked it for porn yet?"

Her blunt question didn't surprise me. In the gaming industry, there was no flinching when it came to casual talk about sex. But the assumption caught me off-guard. "You have people doing that with beta hardware? And you're okay with it?"

"Absolutely. We're encouraging it."

Grayson shook his head. "Haven't gone there yet. It's no fun alone, but if you wanted to send me an extra set or two…" He brushed my hand before slipping his into Jax's.

Heat seared through me at the brief contact.

Lee chuckled. "I'll make a note and see what I can do."

Lee and Grayson chatted a few minutes longer about the hardware specs and upcoming fixes, before she gave us all another smile and headed after someone else.

"You're not really surprised by the porn thing, are you?" Jax asked as we resumed wandering through the crowds.

I shook my head. "Just that they're okay with it."

"They're encouraging indie games and mods from the start." Grayson rested a hand on the small of my back, branding a patch into my skin. "*Company sanctioned* means more control for us over what happens."

That made sense.

"The hardware has other applications too," Jax said.

"Besides jerking off to cartoon people? Are you sure?" I teased. "I know it's already being investigated for military- and medical-training purposes."

Jax led us to the bar and ordered two Cokes and a seltzer with lime.

looking for it

"You're going to raise eyebrows if you're not drinking when there's an open bar. And thank you." I took my soda from him.

The seltzer was for Grayson. He dipped his head to rest his lips near my ear. "Let them talk. We want you sober tonight."

"Applications specifically for you." Jax talked over the questions that tried to bubble up in my head. The demand for answers. "Imagine being able to see a 3D mockup of your outfits before you start sewing, with no more work than what you do now, when you design them in Photoshop."

I liked the thought, and I loved that they were thinking about my work that way. "It's not that simple. Is it?"

Grayson sipped his drink. "Not yet. But it's getting there." He nodded across the room. "The guy over there, with the neon-purple hair? He's the head of digital output at that new studio. The one giving ILM and Weta Workshop a run for their money. He uses the hardware to storyboard."

"They did the effects for the hot new horror movie." I'd heard the guy was insanely brilliant. Like, talked above most people's heads, but came up with such groundbreaking ideas that no one minded. "The combination of digital and physical is supposed to be surreal."

Jax smiled. "That's him. *Supposed to be*? You haven't seen it yet?"

I gave him a look of disbelief smattered with *duh?* I loved horror movies, but Anne and Lyn weren't fans. I'd rather see the spectacular films with friends, so we could all *ooh* and *ah* at the same time, so I usually went with Grayson, but he'd been busy.

"Not yet," I said.

"We should go," Grayson said. "Christmas afternoon?"

"And you might be able to convince me to go." Jax didn't sound enthusiastic.

I was surprised he made the offer at all. "You can hide behind your popcorn during the scary scenes."

"I can squeal in terror and hide my face in your shoulder." Jax mimicked hiding behind me, brushing a light kiss on my shoulder in the process. "As long as you promise not to tell anyone I covered my eyes through half the movie.

A flash of need pulsed between my legs. How much longer did we have to be here? "Everyone already knows."

"Good point. I'm in anyway." Jax straightened again.

Aside from the questions their behavior was planting in my head, about what I was to them, this

looking for it

was nice. Normal. The way things usually were with us.

But those questions bounced against the reminder they were a couple, and regardless of anything else, that wasn't going to change. I certainly couldn't choose between them or push them apart.

It didn't matter how much teasing and flirting there was. I needed to be happy with being a horror-movie buddy. Nothing more.

When Jax and Grayson were pulled into separate conversations, my mind had room to wander. I could either focus on the impending inbox explosions waiting for me on all of my accounts, or direct my attention to what was going on with the guys. It seemed more likely I could act on the second one first, and it was a more pleasant thought.

Grayson said we'd talk about what we all were. How we introduced ourselves to people. That didn't make sense. This wasn't exactly the kind of society where someone said *this is my boyfriend, and this is our fuck buddy.*

Was he talking about me being more to them? I couldn't wrap my brain around that. Sure, they hooked up with other people, but it was never a long-term thing. And yeah, there was polyamory and multiple-person relationships, but those weren't something I could see myself doing.

Aside from the awkwardness of explaining it to Chase, which they seemed a lot more concerned with than I was, I'd also always seen myself as a one-guy girl. It came back to my dream future. Find the perfect guy. Have the perfect wedding. Settle into a life that wasn't perfect, because no life was, but we'd make it work, because we loved each other.

Jax and Grayson had already found their perfect guy, in each other. I was outside fun. I was enjoying it; this definitely wasn't a one-sided arrangement. Did I want to be their booty-call long term, though?

"Sadie?" An unfamiliar voice called my name, startling me, and I turned toward the man. He wasn't anyone I recognized from Rinslet.

"It is you. Wow," he said.

I pasted on a neutral smile. "It is. I'm sorry, I don't recall your name." Was he a colleague of Chase's? Anne's?

"We've never met. I'm Chet." He extended his hand. "I'm a huge fan of your work."

"Thank you." I let some warmth bleed into my expression and returned the handshake. I was cautious about meeting fans in person, especially male fans, but I also appreciated flattery. Grayson and Jax were close enough that I had a back-up escape if needed.

"No. Thank *you*. The way you bring flat drawings to life in a real-world setting is brilliant.

looking for it

That takes some serious talent. I'm not just saying that; I speak from experience."

Possible connection? I never passed on one of those. "Are you in costume design?"

"3D rendering. Our artists struggle to translate 2D into something with depth, and they don't have to do it with fabric." Chet's tone was friendly, and his enthusiasm felt genuine. His gaze never dropped below my neck.

I let the appreciation seep in. "3D rendering fascinates me. There's so much potential in the art form, and we're right on the cusp of crossing the uncanny valley."

"Maybe my team will be the first." He grinned. "I won't keep you long, but when I realized you were here, I wanted to tell you in person, I saw what you posted on your pages this afternoon."

My gut turned itself inside-out. "Oh?"

"It was brave and bold. I'm furious on your behalf that people are doing shit like that. To anyone, and especially to talented artists like you. You have my support."

My heart dislodged from where it was stuck in my throat. "Thank you." I poured my sincerity into my reply.

He gave me another smile. "I'll let you get back to mingling, but good luck. It was a pleasure meeting you."

"Same."

And he was gone, melting into the crowds, like everyone else we'd talked to tonight.

"Do you know who that was?" Jax asked, suddenly by my side again.

"Chet?"

He chuckled. "Charles Stanford. He's Senior Vice President of Art for KaleidoMation."

Dials and knobs clicked in my head, to draw an association. "The 3D-rendering company?" One of the biggest. Even Rinslet bought their assets—CGI models and objects to be used in video games. "Wow. He's a nice guy."

"That's what I hear."

Grayson joined us too. "Do you want to get out of here?"

Was it that late already? I looked at Jax. "Don't you have to stay until things wrap up?" I didn't mind the mingling.

Jax shook his head. "I've done what I need to."

"I'll rephrase the question." Grayson dropped his hand to his pocket and let a hint of black lace peek out. "I keep brushing against these." He dipped his head close to my ear. "Someone's going to notice soon that I'm a walking hard-on, and I'd rather we take you back to our place than hang out here."

Oh. "All right." Any witty reply I had evaporated, but intense, throbbing desire replaced it.

Chapter Twelve

The drive back to the guys' place was painfully basic. Settled between them, warm and safe and very hands-off. It made the anticipation that lingered on the tip of my tongue that much sharper.

Then we were in their bedroom, and Grayson was kissing Jax, their mouths merging and their tongues dancing with such passion, I expected literal sparks. Love flowed and spilled from them in waves.

They broke apart, and Grayson turned to me. He kissed the tips of my fingers. "We talked about who gets to have you first."

"Seems like I should get a say in that decision." I still didn't know how to feel, besides turned on, that they talked about sex with me.

Jax grinned. "That's fair. What's your decision?"

I hadn't expected him to yield so quickly. "Both? Both is good."

"That's where we landed as well." Grayson slid a finger under the neckline of my dress and glided it along my collarbone.

I captured his hand, enjoying the feeling of his skin against mine. "Do I get to see the two of you naked?" These were the pressing questions that needed to be answered.

"Presumably." Amusement lined Grayson's voice.

"You say that, but I keep ending up missing more clothes than either of you." Two times weren't exactly a pattern, but now was the time to balance things out.

Jax pressed into my back. "Are you complaining?"

I liked being a Sadie Sandwich. "About the sex? Not even for a second. About missing out on what I imagine is an incredible view? A little."

"Wouldn't want to ruin the fantasy," Grayson said.

I worked the knot of his tie, to loosen it, then untied it and left the ends hanging loose. "I'm not worried about that."

My world went black when something slipped over my eyes. The texture of silk against my skin said it was Jax's tie, blindfolding me.

I laughed lightly. "Can't see any nakedness this way."

"You will," Jax whispered in my ear.

Shivers raced down my spine, chased by him tugging down my zipper and exposing my back. He

looking for it

pushed my dress to the ground, leaving me on display in the middle of their room, my body screaming in anticipation.

Jax's familiar stubble scraped along my skin when he kissed my shoulder, then nibbled playfully. He trailed a barely-there touch down my spine. Every new contact from him shuddered through my body on a wave of desire.

Where did Grayson go? More than a minute or two couldn't have passed, but the loss of one sense distorted time.

Lips brushed mine. Lightly. Sweetly. Grayson's kiss could have been innocent, if I were wearing more than a pair of heels. He tangled his fingers in my hair and tugged hard, making me gasp. He bit my bottom lip, and licked away the sting.

At the same time, Jax was teasing his fingers lower along my back then slipping between my legs. He caressed my slick skin but didn't part my folds.

Grayson pressed his body to mine. Every texture—fabric, skin, the smoothness and roughness of it all—lit up my senses.

Jax's touch fell away, but Grayson kept my mind and body busy. He glided his touch over my hips, lower, dipping toward my clit but not touching it. Nearly sliding inside me, before pulling away.

Jax was there again, bare skin against my back and his erection digging into me. He gripped my hips and nibbled my ear. "You're not the only one who's been fantasizing, but the reality is much better."

"It really is." My words came out on a gasp. My skin absorbed every sensation, but there was a tug in my chest as well. Jax's words and Grayson's attention warmed me in a way their kisses didn't. They made me want to swoon.

When Grayson's hands fell away, Jax's replaced them. He moved between my legs again, drawing a groan from me when he slipped two fingers inside me. He rested his palm on my stomach, holding me to him. This was more than physical intimacy. It was a feeling I didn't dare look at too closely.

He sought out my clit, dancing lightly at first, but increasing the pressure and speed as my hips bucked into his touch. Climax lingered just out of reach, then flooded through me. I leaned into him, needing the extra support when my legs wobbled. I wanted to memorize everything about this moment.

Jax guided me toward the bed slowly, making sure I didn't trip or run into anything, since I couldn't see. He turned me to lie back on the mattress, my legs hanging over the edge.

When he licked up the inside of my thigh, that scruff of barely-there beard scraped along my skin with a tantalizing burn. I arched into his touch. His open-mouth kisses. Every lick and nip made me

looking for it

squirm a little more. When he reached my core, I whimpered.

He dove in with enthusiasm. His tongue inside me was the only thing I could focus on.

Until Grayson wrapped his lips around my nipple and sucked.

My mind fuzzed, and I let myself fall into it. I lost track of where one touch ended and the next began, and this orgasm lingered just out of reach. When I came, my entire body shuddered.

The blindfold fell away, and Grayson was kissing me.

I blinked rapidly in the abrupt light. "It's bright."

"You wanted to see us," he murmured against my lips.

I had. I took them both in. Grayson, propped up next to me on one elbow, familiar ink trailing down his chest. His cock was large, erect, and wrapped. Jax stood at the foot of the bed, looking just as impressively aroused and sexy as fuck.

Grayson traced the edge of my ear. "How are your legs?"

"Non-functional." Not that I had any issue with that.

"On your side." He nudged me so my back was to him, crooked my leg, and teased my opening with the head of his cock. He glided inside me slowly, stretching me out an inch at a time.

This was a new angle of penetration, and it was an incredible one.

Jax knelt on the mattress in front of me. The way he leaned in, propped up on one knee and arm, was odd. He teased my clit with the head of his cock, then nudged my opening too. They couldn't both… Could they?

"It's like the vibrator. Tell me to stop if it's too much," Jax said.

When he wedged inside me, next to Grayson, the stretch drew a long groan from me.

"You okay?" Jax asked.

I nodded. It hurt, but in a good way. I was so slick and turned on, the pain was delicious. They built to a slow rhythm, rather than the frantic, hard pounding I usually associated with sex. I slipped into pleasure tinged with pain, riding the high of both. When Grayson sought out my clit again, it was too much but just right.

I melted into climax. Mine. Theirs. Ecstasy consumed me.

When they slowed to a stop, there was no subtle pulling out of me. My body contracted when each of them withdrew, but the phantom sensation remained.

looking for it

Grayson held me tight, his heat spreading over me. Jax lay across from me, a silly smile on his lips as he brushed my hair away from my face.

This couldn't last. Not with the kisses I'd seen them share. Not with how much they loved each other. But for now… God, it was incredible.

Chapter Thirteen

Amazing sex and a solid night's sleep between two naked and gorgeous men didn't change the fact that I needed answers.

I was the only one in bed when I woke up, but a faint shuffling sound drew my attention to the closet, where Jax was straightening his tie. He looked good—of course. I could get used to mornings like this.

Another reason to have this conversation now. "Can we talk?"

He jumped, laughed lightly, then met my gaze in the full-length mirror on the back of the closet door. "Morning, gorgeous. I hope I didn't wake you."

"No. I don't think so, anyway."

"It's probably good you're up." He smoothed out his shirt and slacks, and turned to face me. "I have to run into work early. Emergency of some sort. Grayson went to get coffee, but he'll be back soon. He can take you home, or you can hang out here, or whatever you celebrity streamers do while the rest of us are chained to desks."

looking for it

I couldn't hide my exasperation. "Jax."

"Hmm?"

"Are you ignoring my question on purpose?"

He sighed and knelt on the mattress next to me. "No. Sort of, but I heard you."

"Okay. Because I'm having a lot of fun with whatever this is, but I'm not sure how I feel about being your toy." I swore he looked pained when I said *toy*.

"You're not. I promise." He leaned in and brushed his lips over mine. "We'd talk now if I had time. Don't make any decisions until all of us can discuss this together."

Agreeing meant not diving into the conversation with Grayson until Jax was free. But they should both be there, and I didn't want to make Jax late for work. "All right."

Then he was gone, and so was my immediate chance at closure and answers.

Until I could get that, I should go home. Dig into the backlash that waited after my *big reveal* last night.

Slipping into my dress this morning didn't hold the same thrill as last night. Today, the fabric felt like a stretchy sleight-of-hand trick, rather than actual magic. I didn't know what to do with myself, so I took a seat at the kitchen table.

Grayson didn't keep me waiting long. He looked at me with surprise when he stepped into the room, coffees in hand. "You all right?" he asked.

"I should get home. Take care of the fallout from yesterday."

He gave me a cup and kept one for himself. "You could do a lot of that here, if you wanted."

"I can't." As much as I liked the idea of hanging out a little longer.

"Why not?"

A heavy sigh slipped out. "We *all* need to talk, and I'm not sure I can stay away from the topic until then."

"I see. I'll take you home, then."

The ride to my place was quiet. I was desperate to talk about what was happening between us, and since I'd promised to wait, I couldn't think of anything else Grayson and I had ever talked about before this point.

When we pulled up in front of Lyn's house, Grayson handed me my phone.

I reached for the truck door handle.

"Sadie—"

I paused at the catch in his voice and looked at him.

Grayson worked his jaw. "I want to—" He shook head. "You're right. We should all be here for this conversation."

looking for it

Now I was extra curious, but I'd wait. "Yeah. Talk to you soon." I didn't dare look back as I headed inside.

When I reached my room, I turned on my phone and woke up my laptop. My notifications and unread emails were only in the hundreds. Not nearly as bad as the situation could have been.

I mentally rolled my eyes at myself.

"You back?" Lyn called.

"Yeah."

She poked her head into my room. "Some guy dropped this off for you this morning. Everything all right?"

I grabbed the stapled papers from her. *Cease and Desist* was in a neat typeface across the top, next to my name and address. "It will be." I gave her a tight smile.

"Okay. I have to get back to the shop, but holler down if you need anything."

I scanned the C&D and posted it online, along with a series of hashtags, including #wewontbesilenced

I couldn't avoid the messages anymore, so I dug in. They fell into three main categories.

I'm so sorry you got scammed.

They got me too. Thank you for speaking out.

And, *You're a fucking whore. Someone should rape you to death. You don't deserve how good they tried to be to you.*

Most days I loved the internet, but when the assholes came out…

I spent hours replying to the kind words and blocking everyone who sent the cruel ones. It was early afternoon when it weighed down my soul so much, I didn't know if I could breathe.

I couldn't face this onslaught this way. I recorded a quick video, thanking everyone for their support, and followed it up with a note that I would be off social media for the holidays. I'd planned on taking a break over Christmas anyway, and now seemed like a good time to put that plan into motion.

The air was too tight in here. The room too oppressive. I needed to get out and clear my head.

I got in my car and drove. West seemed like a good direction today. Out past the mountains, toward the lake. Maybe beyond it. Maybe I'd go to Wendover and drop fifty bucks in the slot machines. Have a late lunch and a free drink or two.

I'd rather not be inside my head. Talking to someone would help me sift through my thoughts. Anne was stuck in crunch time at work, Lyn was working the shop, and Grayson...

Well, that was the problem, wasn't it?

He'd listened to me talk through breakups before. About whatever asshole I'd let crawl under my skin. He understood. Had his own stories to share. Was I about to become one of them? The girl who couldn't accept a little fun when she had the chance?

I wasn't getting anywhere with this. I cranked the radio to sing along at the top of my lungs. Belting out classic hair metal always made me feel better. As long as I skipped every single song about love and broken hearts.

A loud *bang* sounded over the music, and the steering wheel jerked in my hands.

Chapter Fourteen

I gripped the wheel harder and turned into the skid, trying to regain control. The car came to a crooked stop at the side of the road.

The entire thing only took a few seconds, but it shaved years off my life. I turned down the radio, only to be inundated by the sound of my pulse hammering in my ears.

I took several deep breaths to calm myself, then climbed from the car, to see what happened. My back right tire was a shredded mess of rubber that barely covered the rim.

Blow out. Wonderful. But this was something I could act on, and that was more comforting than it should be.

Spare was in the trunk. I knew how to change the tire. I'd be back on the road in twenty minutes.

And eighteen minutes later, as I lowered the jack with frozen fingers, I was feeling pretty smug.

Until the spare tire hit the pavement, and then dropped another few inches. The bottom looked like a rubber pancake. My spare was flat.

looking for it

"Fuuuuuuuck." I let the day's frustration fill my scream into the air. I shouted again and again, until my voice was hoarse and my lungs begged me to stop.

Okay. I could do this. No big deal. I probably couldn't get an Uber out here in the middle of nowhere. Would the app even let me enter *mile marker 38 on I-80*?

I hated to call my friends while they were working, but I couldn't afford tow truck fees if I had to get my tires replaced.

I dialed Lyn first, then Anne, and wasn't surprised to not get answers.

Chase picked up. "I'm heading into a client meeting. Can I call you back?"

"Yeah." I'd find someone else.

"Sadie? What's wrong?"

If I told him *nothing*, he'd pry until he got an answer, and that would waste everyone's time. "I had a tire blowout, and my spare is wrecked too. But I've still got people to call. Don't worry about it."

"Where are you?" His hurried brushoff had vanished behind concern.

I gave him the closest location I knew of. "But don't miss your meeting for me."

His conflicted growl almost made me smile. "Fine. This won't take long. Text me if you find anyone in the next fifteen minutes. If I don't hear from you, assume I'm on my way."

"All right. And thank you."

Before I could make another call, my phone buzzed with a text from Chase. *Help is on the way.*

I hoped he didn't ditch his clients for me. I settled back in my seat and pulled my coat tight around me. I was at least forty-five minutes away from any help, and while I had a full tank of gas, I wasn't going to keep the engine running the whole time. I needed to strike a balance between not freezing and not burning through my gas. Why had I grabbed the fingerless gloves instead of the full-blown fuzzy mittens?

Out here, away from most of the city lights, it seemed to get dark faster. It was kind of eerie, watching everything vanish into the creeping night.

Headlights flashed in my rearview mirror, then pulled up behind me on the shoulder. *Please let that be Chase or a good Samaritan, and not some creepy creeper.*

They didn't turn their lights off, so I only saw a silhouette approaching. When Jax knocked on my window, I yelped. I was such a dork sometimes.

I grabbed my purse and keys and opened the door.

"You ordered one knight in shining armor?" He grasped my fingertips and helped me from the car.

looking for it

"I definitely called for help. I didn't expect…" Should I be flirty or plain? It didn't matter now; I'd hesitated too long. "You."

Jax gave a deep bow. "At your service. Your fingers are frozen." He grabbed both of my hands and pressed them between his.

Heat seared through my icy skin, and I groaned in appreciation. I looked up to find Jax watching me with an unreadable look.

"I do love the sounds you make when you're content or happy," he said.

Thank God he couldn't see the blush that raced over my skin. A sliver of fear attached to a memory crowded its way into my thoughts and took me a moment to decipher. This wasn't the Jax who I had a friendly relationship with over the last few years. This was the guy who led me on and broke my heart in high school.

But he wasn't. He'd changed, and I'd seen that.

The knowledge didn't stop a whisper of doubt from burrowing under my skin. "We should get going before we both freeze."

"Yeah. Sure." He shook his head. "We'll get someone back out here in the morning to take care of your car. Grayson knows a guy." Jax held his passenger door open for me until I was secure in my seat, then hurried around to slide into the driver's side.

"Right. I'll make arrangements in the morning."

Jax pulled onto the freeway, and we headed toward Salt Lake. "May I bring you home again? Our place?" he asked. "For that conversation we all need to have?"

Right. *The Conversation.* That thing I'd been itching for since this morning, that suddenly loomed more terrifying than any monster. If we did this, how much of our relationship would I destroy?

Not as much as if I let things drag out. I'd hate myself and resent them, if this went on and I got attached before they cut me loose. "Yes."

"That's it? Just *yes*?" He glanced sideways at me.

"It's not. I want to say a lot more. But if I start now, I won't stop, and you were right that we should all be there." We all needed to be on the same page, and saying what I had to was going to be hard enough once. I didn't want to repeat myself.

"Yeah. Of course."

Silence settled between us, except for the faint music coming from his stereo. Almost like a movie, except at this point in a film, we'd probably be hearing some heartbroken ballad by Adele, and not the Blink182 whispering through his speakers.

Basket Case by Green Day popped up next, and I turned up the volume. It was as appropriate a song as any for my mood. Neither one of us moved to turn

looking for it

the music back down for the rest of the drive. Not the most awkward hour-plus ever of my life, but probably in the top ten.

When we got back to their place, Grayson was waiting. The quick kiss they shared was the same one I'd seen hundreds of times, but tonight it was another reminder that part of their life was for them alone, and that wouldn't change.

Grayson gave me a friendly smile. "I hope you didn't freeze out there. Do you want hot chocolate? A blanket?"

His sweet consideration tightened the already-clenching fist around my heart. "I warmed up in Jax's car." Did that sound dirty? "Heated seats and all. Nothing else."

"I didn't say anything." Grayson shrugged.

Jax gave a tight chuckle. "Sounds like us the entire way here."

That was as good an opening as any. "Speaking of… Thank you for comi—" My brain glitched on the unintentional innuendo. "For picking me up. I'm super grateful. I'm also wondering… Can we skip the small talk and get this over with?"

"That's a good idea." Grayson nodded at the couch.

I wasn't ready to sit, and it looked like neither of them was either. Because of us standing around was so much more comfortable. Not.

"It sounds like you have specific thoughts. You first," Grayson said.

How was that fair? Then again, would anything they said make a difference? This was where I cut us off, even if they wanted to keep up the fun. If I set the tone, I might save us a bit of saying things we might regret. "You're both wonderful—in bed and out of it—and this fling, whatever you'd like to call it, is amazing."

Jax opened his mouth, but Grayson rested a hand on his arm.

Not a subtle or unique gesture, but it added more weight to my decision. "But it's not going anywhere. I know that. The two of you are together, and I'm like the side dish. The longer we keep going with the sex, the more likely one of us will get hurt when it ends." The brief speech clawed at my throat.

Jax scowled. Did I steal his thunder by dumping myself?

I crossed my arms in front of my chest, feeling exposed in a decidedly non-delicious way.

"To us, it's not a fling. Or casual fun. Or whatever you're calling it today," Grayson said.

What else could it be?

Jax moved closer to me, lightly grasped my fingers, and pulled my arms down. He didn't let go of my hands as he met my gaze. "I've been attracted to you for a long time. Both of us have. We're not

looking for it

using you. You're not a side dish." He sounded sincere. But once, a long time ago, I'd fallen prey to his false adoration.

I pulled my hands away and shoved them in my pockets. "What about *being discreet?*"

"We didn't plan that morning any more than you did," Grayson said. "We'd talked about you before—we talk about you a lot—and what you are in our life is too important to toss away on *casual fun.*"

I was really starting to hate that phrase. "So we're on the same page." There was no relief in the realization.

"We're really not." Jax reached for me again, flexed his fingers, then dropped his hand. "We're not telling you it's over. We—Grayson and I—want to see where things go with you. As in, dating. A relationship. The kind we don't keep a secret."

"But the two of you are already dating." I wasn't dim. I understood polyamory, loving more than one person, but it wasn't for me. I'd tumbled down that path mentally several times, trying out the weight, seeing if I could do what Jax and Grayson did by letting other people into their lives. I couldn't.

I didn't want to share my *happily ever after*. I wanted the one guy, the one dress, the one wedding... The one ring. That last one should have made me laugh at my own wit, but I was hung up on other things.

Grayson sank onto the edge of the couch. "We are. And we want to see where things go when you're part of that."

"Things don't *go* anywhere. You're together." I'd said that once. I didn't want to repeat myself. "It's not like I'm going to pick one of you and break you up. I couldn't if I wanted to, and that's the last thing I want. Don't get me wrong, I'm loving the sex and the attention, but I'm not... It's not a long-term relationship kind of thing."

"It's absolutely something people do long term." Grayson studied me with those dark eyes I normally wanted to fall into but today made me turn away with uncertainty.

This wasn't supposed to be so difficult. I expected pain, but not for them to argue with me. Why were they doing this? "Other people. Not me."

"What did you think we were doing?" Jax's scowl was back.

At least that was something I knew how to deal with. It was a hint to summon my emotional armor and close him off from anything I felt. But the wall I put up cracked. "Not every hookup ends in a relationship. I was having fun. I said exactly that. I got the impression both of you were as well."

looking for it

"So we're back on that. *Casual fun.*" Jax spat the words out with frustration.

Something we agreed on. "I feel like you're not hearing me."

"That makes three of us," Grayson said.

"It's not…" Frustration bubbled up in my chest and pricked the inside of my eyelids. "I'm trying to be clear and plain about this. I don't expect that every guy I date is someone I'm going to spend the rest of my life with. That doesn't make the time with them any less enjoyable."

"We're already spending most of our lives together." Jax took a seat, but not next to Grayson.

That should be better. It didn't give the impression of them standing against me. But now I was on trial, with them judging me because I wanted something different from my future than they saw. "Because we're friends. I'm not planning on pledging my love—not the way you're talking about—to Lyn or Anne either."

"But have you slept with them?" Jax asked.

I glared. What the fuck kind of question was that?

"You're not even willing to consider this." Grayson's tone had shifted to an irritation that I never heard from him. "In that case, doesn't that make us the fuck dolls? You had your fun, you got to be naughty, and now you're done and move on?"

Fuck dolls. Horrible phrase. "You're putting words in my mouth."

"We're trying to understand." Grayson spoke through clenched teeth.

"So am I. I don't see why you think this is going to work when I'm telling you it's not for me."

"What did you think was going to happen?" Jax's question bled accusation. "Or didn't you? Did you approach us like everything else in your life, diving in without thought, and enjoying what happens now, fuck the consequences?"

The bitterness in his words felt like a slap, and I fumbled for a response. He saw me that way?

Chapter Fifteen

"This conversation is over." Grayson crossed the room to the stand by the front door, and grabbed his keys. "I'll take you home."

"Everyone wanted to talk. Let's finish talking." Jax didn't move, and that included the glare he had fixed on me.

"I agree." I stared back with as much ice as I could muster. "I want to know what you meant."

Jax was on his feet now too. He stalked toward me, stopping when his nose was inches from mine, anger flashing on his face. "You're in your current place, staying with Lyn, because you let your lease run out. You're heading off to Hollywood on a whim, without any thoughts of what you're leaving behind—"

"*On a whim?*" I was only a few decibels from shouting. "I think you mean *pursuing my dream*. You know, that thing I've worked toward for years. Growing my skills, building a fan base, and making connections. That *whim*? I'm not leaving anything behind, because my friends, the ones who don't try to emotionally manipulate me into giving up something I love, will keep in touch."

Grayson sighed. "He didn't mean—"

"Oh. My. God." I turned my frustration on him. "How often are you going to say that? Maybe if Jax doesn't mean things, he should stop saying them." Like calling me a *girl in tacky outfits*. The memory surged back on a rush of bile and lodged in my throat. I swallowed it as best I could. "You're right. It's time for me to go." If I kept talking, none of this would be salvageable. Maybe it wasn't anyway.

"I think that's a good idea." Grayson reached for the door.

I brushed past him. "Stay here. I'll call someone." *Who tries to understand me.*

Was I as guilty of that as they were?

I didn't know. I did know it hurt when Grayson closed the door behind me, leaving me in the cold. Why couldn't I just give them what they wanted?

Because that wasn't who I was. And now it had thrown up a huge divider between us.

I could knock. Ask for a chance to make things right. But I said what I meant to. There might not be a *right* in this case. And it might have cost me good friends.

I grabbed my phone to call for a ride, and found a message waiting from Anne. *Did you make it home*

looking for it

*all right? Work's over. Let me know if you need
anything.*

*Actually, I'm at the guys' house. Can you come
get me?* It was a plain message that would raise a
dozen questions. I'd answer them when she got here.

Her reply buzzed through seconds later. *Of
course. On my way.*

I was sitting on the curb, using the cold concrete
to numb my thoughts as effectively as it did my ass,
when Anne pulled up.

"What happened?" she asked as soon as I slid
into the car.

Where to start? "Jax..."

"I'm going to kick his ass." Anne reached for
the door.

I grabbed her other arm. "Don't. It's not like
that."

"Did he hurt you?"

Yes. "I think I hurt them first. I don't... I can't
even make sense of it, to put it into words."

"That's not like you."

"I know, right?" I sank down in my seat. "I
think I fucked up, but I'm not sure. It felt right at the
time. Now it just hurts."

Anne pulled onto the road. "At the time?"

"All of fifteen minutes ago." I tried to laugh.
"*Fuck.* Maybe he's right. Maybe. I am only capable
of living in the moment."

"That's not true. What do you need?"

"I need… to not talk about it." It hurt too much to even think about, and my confusion muddied everything. "How did work go?"

Anne tugged on her hair. "We pushed back the deadline. We're not going to make it before the holidays."

She'd put way too many hours into their latest game, fighting to make it work amid setbacks and incompetence. Having the game pushed back had to be a slap in the face to Anne's hard work.

"I'm sorry." I'd rather focus on making her feel better. "Sounds like we both need an escape."

One corner of Anne's mouth tugged up. "Shopping?"

"The only place open this late is Walmart."

"Online." The *duh* in her voice was playful.

I liked that. "For board games?"

"Craft supplies."

Inspiration sparked in my head. Perfect distraction. "Craft supplies, to make board games."

"Who has to come up with the rules?" Anne's voice was lighter.

"Every game will be different. We'll make the rules up as we go." And Jax's words were back, both in high school and tonight. Taunting me for being awkward, impulsive, and not caring how my decisions impacted people.

looking for it

Anne glanced at me. "Lord of the Rings marathon."

Thank God for intuitive friends. "Don't you have to work in the morning?"

"We get the weekend off."

First time in two months. It had to feel good and frustrating at the same time. "Extended edition it is."

Anne's place was a small house near downtown. A single floor with two bedrooms, a kitchen, and a living room. The brick exterior belied what was inside.

She'd converted one of the rooms into a theater-slash-gaming room. Chase, Anne, and I had spent a weekend soundproofing the place after she bought it, so she could turn up the bass without bothering the neighbors.

We settled into two recliners, a bowl of popcorn between us, and started *Fellowship*.

Anne was asleep before they reached Rivendell. It was good to see her getting some rest.

I wouldn't be anytime soon. I turned down the volume, but left the movie playing while I made myself some coffee. We'd both seen it so many times, it didn't matter what we missed.

Hot drink in hand, I settled back into my seat and tried to focus on the costumes. They were my favorite part of these films. So much incredible detail and hard work went into every piece. I loved studying them and working out the techniques that had been used.

I couldn't focus on them tonight, though. My fight with Grayson and Jax kept charging back into my thoughts.

I wanted to see their perspective. Tried picturing myself with both of them. Tonight was devouring me; it hurt to for them to take a position against me. How much worse would that be if we tried to be together romantically?

What happened if I got closer to Grayson than Jax?

My mind revolted on that thought too.

I didn't see any solutions. Only an endless loop of questions.

Chapter Sixteen

"You want coffee?"

Three of the sexiest words ever dragged me from sleep. I opened one eye to find Anne perched in the chair next to mine. She held out a mug with Ms. PAC-MAN on it.

I forced myself the rest of the way to consciousness and took the offering. Near-scalding liquid slid down my throat. "You really do love me."

"Always."

"What time is it?" Sunlight streamed through the cracks in the heavy curtains.

"Almost noon," Anne said. "You looked too cute, sleeping. I didn't want to wake you up, but Lyn texted. Someone called in sick, and she needs help with the Christmas rush."

Great excuse to immerse myself in socializing and ignore a problem I didn't have an answer for. "I'm in. Wait. Why are you in?"

Anne wasn't as fond of people as I was. She stood with a shrug. "I'm not going to turn down a plea for help. And she said I can mostly stick to kitchen and barista duty."

"That's fair."

I took a few more minutes to wake up, and we were on our way. A brief glance at my phone fractured my creeping good mood. A few missed calls and an ass-ton of emails, none of them from Grayson or Jax. What did I expect, though?

I apologized to Anne for tuning her out while I dialed into my voicemail.

"Ms. Hughes, this is Gregory London, Esquire." An unfamiliar man's voice greeted me. "I represent Ms. G and her associates. You've failed to respond to our cease and desist and have posted further inflammatory slander since. If you don't comply with our request, there will be dire consequences."

Fuck. Could he do that? It had only been a day. They were calling me already? That didn't seem right.

I itched to delete the message and pretend I hadn't heard it. Instead, I saved it in case I needed it later.

"Hi, Mercedes." The next message started off more chipper. "I represent Mr. Watanabe's office. Due to recent events, we're no longer able to meet with you, to discuss employment."

looking for it

Bile rose in my throat, and that message got an instant delete. It was regarding one of the interviews I had lined up for Costume Designer. I had half a dozen others, though. One down wasn't a big deal.

Email was next. Make that three down, thanks to another two cancellations waiting for me. Why were all these people working on a Saturday? Couldn't they wait until Monday, or maybe after Christmas, to band together to crush my dreams?

Lyn's café was packed, which was nice to see. Not a lot of people were gaming, but dozens were buying snacks and trinkets. If she could keep up even half this pace after the holidays, she'd be on track to recover more quickly, financially.

I threw myself into working the register and chatting up customers, but my smile was painted on and I couldn't keep my thoughts from straying toward Jax, Grayson, and my deteriorating future.

When Grayson called, a spark of hope flashed inside. I was in the middle of helping a woman decide between the Minecraft and Pokémon bento boxes for her son, so I couldn't answer.

The instant I was free, I pulled up his message.

"Hey." His voice was flat. "Grabbed your car this morning. Tire's fixed. Let me know when I can drop it off." He had a spare key, the same way Anne did, for when I locked my keys in the car.

Guilt churned inside. My flat was so far down on my list of concerns today, I'd almost forgotten about it. And he'd gone out of his way to make sure I was set, despite last night's disagreement.

Calling him back would have to wait, but I did send him a quick *thank you* text.

The rest of the day passed without a response. I was painfully grateful when Lyn ushered out the last customer and locked the door behind them.

She grabbed my arm and pulled me back into the café kitchen. "Where were you today?" Her voice was kind as she nudged me into a chair.

"Nowhere. Everywhere." Still uncertain where to start.

Anne joined us. "Something happened with Jax and Grayson last night."

I wasn't upset with her for saying so. It was as good an opener as any.

"I'm guessing this wasn't the sexy kind of *something*." Lyn moved around the kitchen as she spoke, pulling plates from one spot and pastries from another. "You know, if you don't talk through it, you're going to drive yourself nuts." She knew me well.

I picked at the cheese Danish she put in front of me, and at a loose thread of last night's conversation. The story tumbled out in a rapid-fire mess of emotion. As I reached the end, the relief I wanted

looking for it

wasn't there. "Was this my fault?" It seemed like it, from an outside perspective.

"You can't change how you feel about the situation, just because they feel differently," Anne said.

Lyn tapped a nail on the edge of her plate. "I'm with her. If loving two people that way isn't for you, then it isn't for you."

Confirmation. Agreement. Why wasn't I reassured?

"This is making you miserable, though." Anne was sympathetic.

"It's like one of you being mad at me. It sucks." At least that was an easy emotion for me to zero in on. "Jax and I… That's always been weird. But Grayson? I fucked things up because I fucked them. I want to go back to the way things were, but I'll always be thinking about… them."

"You fantasize about them, anyway." Anne's food sat untouched in front of her.

In fact, except for the tiny flakes I'd picked from mine, none of us were eating. I took a big bite of the pastry. As the sugar hit my tongue, my stomach grumbled. Maybe I should have consumed something besides coffee between popcorn and now. In a few bites, my dessert was gone. My problems… not so much. "But now I have reality to compare it to."

"Unless the reality was bad, that makes the fantasies that much more vivid. Do you want to make things right with them, as friends?" Lyn slid me her Danish.

I should have insisted she eat it. But it wasn't as though it was the last one in the kitchen. I consumed it more slowly. "Yes."

"There's your answer." Lyn made things sound simple.

Anne shook her head. "It's not that easy."

"I need to call them. Or head over there." I didn't want to try to mend our friendship over the phone, and I could pick up my car. I looked at Anne. "Drop me off?"

"All right." She pushed her plate to Lyn. "Eat this. No arguments. It will taste better than salad."

"What about you?" Lyn asked.

Anne grinned. "I may have helped myself to a couple while I was back here today. I'm Danished out."

Despite my mood, that drew a laugh. I promised Lyn I'd let her know if I was going to be delayed for whatever reason, texted Grayson to say I wanted to talk if they were there, and was on my way with Anne.

She pulled up in front of their house and squeezed my hand. "We're here if you need anything."

looking for it

"Thank you." I knew it—I'd do the same for her or Lyn—but hearing it was reassuring.

I strode up the front walk with my back straight and my thoughts racing. My apology and request hovered on the tip of my tongue, rewriting themselves an infinite number of times with each step I took.

The door opened before I knocked. Grayson stepped aside to let me in, and closed the door behind me.

Jax stood a few feet away, in the living room, and joined him.

The atmosphere was so heavy, I could choke on it. Instead, I lingered in the entryway, back and palms pressed to the door. The cool steel pressed into my skin, giving me a place to focus.

"I'm sorry for overreacting," I said. That wasn't so hard. Then again, it was the easiest thing I had to say. "I let the heat of the moment get to me."

Jax cleared his throat, staring at his feet. "I'm sorry too." He looked up. "I was hurt, and I didn't mean the things I said."

I dragged in a deep breath, to steady my thoughts more than anything. "I did. For the most part I meant all of it. I adore you both, but I'm not a two-guy girl. I can't see myself sharing my love like that." It hurt to say. I loved them the way I loved any of my friends, but romantically? I couldn't do that.

Grayson worked his jaw a few times, and I braced myself for Round Two of last night. "So now what?" he asked.

Now I said the rest of what I came to, and hoped it didn't cost me too much. "I want… Can we still be friends?"

"Yes." Jax's answer was instant.

So far so good.

"Maybe, eventually." Grayson's reply was a knife through my heart. "I need time, and I don't know if we can ever go back to what we were."

Anger rose inside, fueled by hurt. "So you were only ever friends with me for the hope of more?" The instant the words passed my lips and his face twisted to match what I felt inside, I wanted to rethink my approach.

"No." Grayson's voice was stone. "But we both made assumptions, and some of those can't be taken back. I can't pretend I'm okay, any more than you can step into a relationship that doesn't feel right to you."

"Fine." I reached for the doorknob.

"Sadie." Grayson's voice sent a shred of hope through me. I looked at him, not daring to say anything. He handed me my spare car key. "Probably give this to someone else, to hold onto."

looking for it

And that was that. I closed my fingers around the cold metal, the teeth biting into my skin. That was that.

Chapter Seventeen

Staying off social media for the couple of days leading up to Christmas was easier than I expected.

Not picking up the phone and calling Grayson when I wanted to head out to breakfast Christmas Eve was excruciating.

Every single interview I had lined up with Hollywood costume designers fell through. One even told me if I wormed my way into the industry under a different name, I needed to remember what a close-knit community they were, and that they wouldn't tolerate someone bullying them.

I was the bully. Right.

I hadn't lost everything. Not even close. I still had friends. My family. My channel. And it was Christmas—my favorite holiday of the year. My parents had gone on a cruise this year, but Chase and I would still have lunch at their house. He was cooking, and he liked their kitchen better than his own.

And Anne would be there, the way she had been for almost as long as I could remember. Her home

looking for it

life had been dark and painful when she was a kid. Mom and Dad made sure she had an escape, and that included spending Christmas with us.

Jax and Grayson would be there too. I was ambivalent about seeing them again. Which was why I was lying on my bed, memorizing the patterns in my wallpaper and the way my holiday lights cast shadows, rather than getting ready for lunch.

"You still here?" Lyn knocked.

I sat up. "Yeah. Come in."

She stepped into my room. We'd exchanged gifts last night, and she was wearing the empire waist blouse I'd made her and a drug-store Santa hat. She was heading to her family's house for the rest of the day. "I'm out of here. Do you need anything?"

Answers. Direction. A way to make things right with Grayson and Jax. "I'm good."

"Okay." She didn't sound convinced. "I left a tray of treats on the kitchen table, for you to bring. Tell everyone I said *Merry Christmas*."

I forced a smile. "Thank you. Tell Hollie and Alex the same." I hadn't made cookies to send her parents, but I did make sure she had a bottle of their favorite whiskey.

"I will." Lyn hesitated. "Are you sure…"

I climbed from my bed. "I appreciate everything. Go. Have fun. I'll see you tonight."

She left, and I needed to be on my way too. I should have gone half an hour ago.

My parent's house was only fifteen minutes away. Ten minutes, when the roads were this empty. The other cars were in the driveway when I arrived. I steeled myself. Things had been awkward with Jax at these things a few years ago, when he and Chase started talking again. This wouldn't be much different, and I could spend most of my time with Anne.

I didn't want it to work that way, but if the situation was too tense, that was the plan.

"Hey." Anne saw me the instant I stepped inside, and she joined me. "Chase was about to send out the search parties."

"Sorry about that. I was... Stuff." Wow. Brilliant, me.

She took the bag of gifts that hung from my right arm. "I'll put these under the tree."

I gave her a grateful smile, and retreated to the kitchen to stash the treats from Lyn.

Chase gave me a quick hug and pointed me toward the dining room. I was late enough that it was time to eat.

I sat next to Anne, disappointment swelling inside when Grayson refused to make eye contact with me. Jax spared me a glance, but nothing more.

looking for it

The food was incredible. Not that I was surprised. Chase managed to outdo himself every year. The conversation—or lack thereof—was excruciating. It was limited to Anne and Chase, talking about the game Rinslet was pushing back, and everyone else occasionally asking someone to pass the salt or butter.

Grayson had barely finished eating, when he pushed back from the table. "We need to get going. Thanks for a great dinner."

"Whoa." Chase's exclamation was painfully loud, compared to the silence it shattered. "What's going on?"

Jax shrugged. "Nothing."

Chase looked at me.

"Nothing." Apparently. The guys hadn't wanted Chase to know before. They sure as fuck wouldn't be interested in filling him in now. Not that I wanted to, either.

He looked at Anne. "Don't suppose you know."

"Nope." I wouldn't have him drag her into an argument that had nothing to do with her beyond her being my confidant. "Nothing means nothing."

"Except it's not *nothing*," Chase said. "Someone's got an issue with someone, and I want to know why."

"Why? Why is it any of your fucking business? Why has it ever been?" Jax's retort was harsh.

The surprise on Chase's face matched what I felt. "Because we're all family. Aren't we?" he said.

"I wouldn't assume anything of the sort." Grayson gripped the back of his chair, a visible tremor running through his hands.

His words scraped across my already raw nerves. True, I'd turned down their offer to see where things went, but he hadn't exactly been up front about his intentions when this entire hookup thing started. "I don't know why you expect anyone else not to make assumptions. Seems a bit hypocritical to me," I said.

"People seeing the world differently than you do isn't hypocrisy; it's reality," Grayson fired back.

The way he twisted my words cranked my anger a notch higher. "And it's also not my fault. Are you going to guilt me into changing my mind? Pull some sort of *I was just being a nice guy* bullshit?"

Grayson's face shifted to that stony cold expression I was learning to dread, and he clenched his jaw.

"Nice guy…" Chase trailed off. "Did you… With one of them?"

"Both." I bit off the word. "And Jax is right. Since when is it your business who I hook up with?"

"Don't drag me into this after pushing us away." Jax's voice held a hash edge. "You're not even fucking interested. After all that."

looking for it

"How does it feel?" My retort slipped out before my brain caught up.

Jax stared at me. Then again, everyone was staring at everyone. Poor Anne looked like she wanted to crawl under the table and hide.

"What are you talking about?" Jax asked.

The past I'd tried to pretend for so long was behind me, came rushing back. That frozen instance of— "Being led on. Having to find out from someone else that you convinced the girl in the tacky outfits that you liked her." Repeating the words tasted foul. Reliving that moment when Chase told me … The scars were fresher than I expected.

"You sound like you're referencing a specific thing, but I have no idea what you're talking about." Confusion bled in Jax's anger.

My hurt grew. "Of course you don't remember. Chase overheard you, back in high school. It's why he stopped talking to you for so many years?"

"Umm…"

"*I* stopped talking to *him*"—Jax cut Chase off— "because he told me not to date you, and I told him it was none of his business who I went out with."

The pretty story now didn't change what happened then. "Because you were leading me on."

"About that…" Chase worked his jaw.

"Because I was falling in love with you," Jax shouted.

Wha… The bottom dropped out of my reality, and my insides pooled in my feet. "But Chase said—"

"He wouldn't back off." Chase sounded sheepish. "So I made something up. I didn't think you still remembered."

He didn't think— "Do you have any idea how much that hurt me?" Tears clogged my throat, but I wouldn't break down here.

"It was a decade ago. You're friends now, so I figured you were over it," Chase said.

Anne smacked him on the arm. "What the fuck is wrong with you?"

Jax was still staring at me. "I can't believe you thought I'd say that about you."

"Who was I supposed to believe? My brother, or the guy he overheard talking shit about me? Besides, you apologized."

"Because you were upset. I wanted you back, and I didn't know what I'd done."

Fuck. I didn't even know which way was up right now.

"We're gonna go." Grayson's knuckles were still curled and pale when he let go of the back of the chair.

Chase nodded. "I think that's a good idea."

"No one asked you what you thought. At all." Anne rarely sounded so angry. "You're the last

looking for it

person who should ever have anything to say about this. *Ever.*"

"Except maybe me." Because I had no clue what I thought or felt anymore. "You guys do whatever you want. I'm going home." My brother had lied to me. I'd been hiding for years from an attraction I didn't want to deny, and harboring a grudge in the process. And my heart felt like a gaping chasm was running through it.

Chapter Eighteen

I expected to cry on the way home, but the tears weren't there. *I was falling in love with you.* At least the Jax voice in my head was saying something different than it had for years. My own brother said… I'd been mad at Chase for a lot of things, but this one had me seeing red. And Grayson was, apparently, a *friendzone* asshole.

Not true. Part of me recognized he was hurt and struggling, like I was.

What was I supposed to do? Life had gone from just the right dash of chaotic to completely fucked up in such a short amount of time. I hated it. I was tired of not knowing where my future was, what I wanted, who I wanted to be with, or where I was going.

Lyn wasn't back when I got home. She would probably be out for a few more hours. I hoped her day was the polar opposite of mine.

The empty house felt like an expansion for my rambling thoughts. I headed up to my room and closed the door, to see if confining everything would help.

looking for it

It didn't.

I sank into the chair in front of my computer, and screamed wordlessly until my breath ran out. Then I inhaled and started again.

My thoughts were still as much of a wreck as my life. I needed control. To do *something*, anything, that I had power over.

My phone buzzed. A text from Chase. I deleted it without reading it. I couldn't deal with him. With what he'd done. It didn't matter that it was so long ago. The discovery—the hurt—was fresh.

And I wouldn't let myself think about Jax or Grayson. That was the path toward a swirling pool of insanity, because I had no answers.

I also refused to wallow and do nothing. Next year's design schedule was open, in anticipation of my picking up and moving. Time to fix that. I'd create new, more unique than ever designs, and fuck being stonewalled by Hollywood—I'd find another avenue for my future. I'd redefine everything.

I grabbed my sketchpad and colored pencils, rolled my chair to the clear part of my desk, and started to sketch. This was a project I'd wanted to do for years, a custom piece of female armor, but it wasn't work and it wasn't pressing, so I'd been putting it off.

Today I poured everything into it. Notes about textures. Fabric. Shapes.

Anne texted me. *You all right?*

I sent her back a quick *Yes :)* and kept my focus on my work.

Chase sent me another message, and then called. I ignored it all. The horror-movie date with Grayson and Jax was presumably off. Assumptions let things go this far. What was one more?

I lost track of time as I spilled different angles and dozens of notes onto one page after another. Then I moved onto a male version. A rough sketch. I wanted to see them together. I turned to a fresh page and let my pencils fly over the paper.

Who was I going to have model this for me? The picture in front of me blurred. I scrubbed away the tears with the back of my hand, and turned the page. Time for a different outfit. Something white. Maybe with gold accents. The faintest pink. Lace.

The rough outline of a wedding dress stared back at me. Forget worrying about two grooms; I didn't even have one.

I ripped the page from my sketchpad, crumpled it up, and tossed it at the wall. It hit without a sound and dropped to the floor just as silently

"Sadie." Lyn's quiet voice yanked me from whatever I was stuck in.

I looked up, to find her standing next to my desk, studying me with concern. I tried to grin, but it

looking for it

came out more like a grimace. "Hey. How was your Christmas?"

"A lot better than yours, from what Anne tells me. What can I do?"

"Nothing. What's done is done." I flipped back to the armor I'd started on. "I need some opinions about this."

"Of course." Rather than looking at my sketchpad, Lyn crossed the room and picked up the crumpled page I'd tossed away. She smoothed it out against her leg, then looked at me. "This is gorgeous."

I clenched my jaw and tried to collect my thoughts. "That's not what I'm working on." My voice cracked.

Lyn returned to crouch next to me, to look me in the eye even as I stared at the carpet. "Tell me," she said.

Talking about that wouldn't accomplish anything. I showed her the armor. "What do you think of this?"

She took my sketchpad from me, set it on the desk, and tugged me to sit next to her on the edge of the bed. Without my distraction in front of me, the rest of the day was free to rush back in.

"What if I never get to wear one?" The worry tumbled out without my permission. "It's a stupid question. It's not like I won't date other guys."

Except the thought made my stomach churn. "And yeah, I can make one any time, but what if I never get to wear one for the intended purpose?" It was only one piece of my plan for the future, but it had been the impetus for so much else, and with my plans crumbling around me…

"What are we assuming is the intended purpose?"

I looked at her skeptically.

Lyn gave me a tiny smile. "Humor me. Answer the question."

"Getting married. Obviously being someone's wife isn't going to define me, but a girl has her dreams."

"Getting married is a lot of things to a lot of different people. For instance, I don't see you as someone who will be happy purchasing a license and letting a justice of the peace process you in the next room over. Where the only thing that says *we're married* will be signing your name on a piece of paper."

That sounded horrible. So bad, it almost made me smile. "No. That's not me."

"You want an outdoor ceremony on the lawn, in the sunshine. You and your girls in gorgeous dresses. The guys in matching tuxes. Everyone's friends and family, watching you declare your love

looking for it

for each other. Celebrating a moment no one else will ever have, because your love is yours and unique.”

It was a painfully beautiful description, and it refractured my heart. My brain wanted to put either Jax or Grayson across from me, and at the same time, the *either-or* of the thoughts ached. “What if that’s not an option for me?”

“Why wouldn’t it be?”

“Because three people can’t get married.” Saying it aloud released a cork on my fears. They had a shape now, which made them sound silly and more terrifying at the same time.

Lyn shook her head. “Not in the first scenario, they can’t. The state’s not super flexible about that. But in the second—your dream wedding—why not?”

What about jealousy? And feeling left out? And everything that came with being a third wheel? “Because… it doesn’t work that way.” A weak answer, but it was all I had.

“Maybe not. But maybe it does.” Lyn hugged me. “Come downstairs. I’ll eat brownies if you will.”

Brownies weren’t a solution, but my thoughts spun in a different direction now, looking at things from an angle I couldn’t see before, and chocolate sounded like a good way to help that along.

Chapter Nineteen

Talking to Lyn didn't help me sort my thoughts so much as it lodged ideas in my head that I'd dismissed before. Which meant my brain was more of a mess than ever.

I was going to adjust my plan for the future. The career part of it.

But none of the plan stood alone. Thinking about my career goals led back to thoughts of love, and I couldn't see anyone but Jax and Grayson in that picture. The same old argument was there—it couldn't work. I couldn't share and be happy. But now I couldn't imagine it working any other way, with any other guy, either.

It was jumping the gun, to even take the thought that far. They wanted to see where things went, and I was planning the rest of my life around the idea. Then again, that was the only way to look at it. Sure, I didn't plan on marrying every guy I dated, but the possibility was there for each one.

And with them…

I couldn't linger in that corner.

looking for it

Telling myself to stop thinking about Jax and Grayson was like ordering someone not to think about an elephant. Completely counterproductive. "When did this all start?" I asked my empty room.

With the sex was the easy answer. But they'd been thinking about it—about me in that way—before then, or Jax wouldn't have made the proposal. I wouldn't have accepted if the fantasies didn't already exist.

With both of them, regardless of what I told myself.

"When did it all start to fall apart?" The walls weren't going to give me answers, but asking the questions aloud helped me feel better. It dragged me out of my own head.

With the sex. Maybe. At the RinCon courtesy suites? That was when I started to put pieces together. Amid talk of hacking VR for porn and turning costumes 3D with rendered assets. When I couldn't ignore what was right in front of me any longer.

"Wait. What?" I rewound, and landed on my conversation with Chet. *Our artists struggle to translate 2D into something with depth.* "No…"

But yes. It was brilliant. What if his artists didn't have to imagine it? What if someone gave them a real-life model to work from? Maybe they already did that. Was that a thing? Could it be my thing?

I'd make it mine. I found contact information for Charles Sanford on the KaleidoMation website, but it was a generic email. I wanted to get to him directly and crossed my fingers he was as big a fan as he'd said.

I sent Anne a quick message, asking if she knew anyone at work who could help me out, then dove into my proposal. I'd want to start with a simple email, to request a meeting. Then something brief— a high-level overview, including a few portfolio shots but mostly a discussion of the concept. And a third that dove into details.

A reply came in to my message to Anne, but it was from Jax. Seeing his name in my email twisted me into a pretzel. The message itself, a digital copy of Chet's business card, complete with a personalized email address, was as benign as could be.

I typed a dozen different replies, before settling on *thank you*.

My letter for Chet was ready. Send it now, the day after Christmas, and take a chance on it getting lost in all the messages he'd get over the holiday, or hold onto it?

looking for it

Who was I kidding? I couldn't sit on this for a week. I gave the thing another proofread and hit *Send*. Now I'd wait.

What next?

Talking to Grayson and Jax. I needed things to be right between us, and chasing them around in my head wasn't getting us there. I could also return Chase's messages, but I wasn't ready to forgive him.

I sent Grayson and Jax a shared message, asking if we could talk.

Grayson's reply came through seconds later. *Can't. Busy this week.*

Oh. There was no room there to pick a date—set a time at some point in the future. Just a *nope*.

I couldn't leave it at that. *My schedule is flexible. When are you free?*

Can't say, Grayson replied.

Jax's silence was at least as bad as Grayson's stonewalling. What were my options? Showing up to their house unannounced. But that was rude, and it also showed I didn't believe Grayson's *busy*. I wasn't sure if I did or not, but implying he was a liar wouldn't help the conversation.

I needed to give them a more concrete request. An invitation with a specific date and time, that didn't leave any room for guessing about when they were busy. They had plans for New Year's, but what if I could make things right and recreate that missed moment with Jax, way back when? Reset that first misunderstanding, when Chase tried to tear us apart? Except Grayson would be there, too, and I could show the both that I wanted the in my life.

I'd give it a day before I sent the request. Let them simmer on things, the way I'd been doing.

Another *ping* from my email derailed my thoughts. A reply from Chet. That had to be a good sign.

Sadie,

It's great to hear from you. I'm definitely interested in your proposal. If you have something you can email, send it over, and I'll get back to you.

I've been watching the public side of your legal situation. I hope things are all right on that front.

I need to talk to some people here before I can get you more of an answer.

Was this his polite way of brushing me off? He was being kinder about it than anyone in Hollywood. I sent my proposal over, as requested, but with his mentioning my legal issues, I didn't expect I'd ever hear back.

Chapter Twenty

Grayson accepted my invitation for the night before New Year's Eve, on both of their behalves. It felt a little silly to make an appointment to visit them, but if this was what it took to make things right…

Was that an option?

God, I hoped so.

I wanted to dress up fancy. Relive that moment Jax and I never got in high school, but better since Grayson would be there, with the blue dress to match my eyes, and the jewelry to match theirs. Once things were better.

Instead, I went for casual but neat, in jeans and a flattering sweater, and now I stood on their porch, both relieved and terrified to finally be knocking.

Grayson answered. No smile. No expression I could interpret.

My heart cracked at seeing him again.

"Come on in." He stepped aside. One obstacle down. "It's just me. Do you want anything to drink?"

"I'd love to be drinking heavily right now." I laughed. He didn't join in. Noted. I wouldn't make any more drinking jokes. Jax was here—his car was in the driveway—but I'd say this twice or three times or a million if I had to. "I need you to know I'm sincere, though, so no thanks."

I did sit. Perched on the edge of a chair, trying not to look like I was ready to bolt. I'd never felt more uncomfortable here.

Grayson reclined on the couch, watching me warily. "What's up?"

"I thought we were going to be okay."

"No you didn't. Too many things were said. Too much hurt was passed around."

"I'm not done," I said. "When I asked if we could be friends, I'd convinced myself we could be okay. Before that, when we hooked up, I let myself believe it wasn't a big deal. I did know better, but it was easier to listen to the voice that wanted the world without offering anything in return."

Grayson raised his eyebrows.

A facial expression. I'd take it. "I'm sorry." Now that the words were flowing, they tasted better than any words had in ages. They didn't have the same foul bitterness of everything else I'd tried to pretend was real. "I'm sorry I couldn't understand what you were asking from me. I'm sorry I pushed you away because I couldn't see what could be— only what couldn't. I want to take it all back, and I

looking for it

know that's not an option. But I want to do things differently now."

"You thought you knew what you wanted before. Why should I listen? What makes this any different?"

Harsh questions, but fair. "I can't make you hear me out. One of the things I've always adored about you is that you're forgiving. That you allow people to learn and grow, and you understand changing an opinion based on new input."

"Tell me what you want to say." His voice wasn't as flat as before.

Skip all the drawn-out explanations and get to the point? Where was the fun in that? I kept the sarcastic thought to myself. I crossed the room, to kneel at his feet. I needed to look him in the eye for what came next, and this was the best way to ensure he would meet my gaze. "I want you back in my life. Both of you. I want to see where things go. I don't want to pretend this is just fun and games and *casual.*"

I swore he was trying to peer into my soul. He was welcome to see it. I'd lay myself out bare, inside and out, to make them understand.

"Don't say any of this simply to make things right." Grayson leaned in, bringing his face closer to mine. "I need you to mean what you're saying."

That was fair. "I mean all of it. Yes, I miss you, and I thought a lot about how to bridge the divide between us. But I'm not going to make up something I don't feel—especially something like this—to put a fake bandage on the situation."

Something rustled behind me, possibly coming from the kitchen. Was Jax listening?

"I've been thinking about this—about us—for a long time. Fantasizing. Asking myself how two people who loved each other could share… It's been in my head for years, but I never looked too deeply into the why. When you told me you wanted me to be a part of that… I needed a new perspective, once everything started to come together. I'm sorry it hurt you, but I can't apologize for taking time to figure it out. That is what it is."

Grayson rested a finger under my chin, lifted my head, and brushed his lips over mine. It was a feather-light touch, but it still sent a shock crashing over me, like shoving icy skin under scalding water.

It ached all the way to my core, but I didn't want to pull away from the relief.

"I'm sorry." I didn't know what this apology was for. It didn't matter, if it earned me more tenderness and understanding.

"It's not your fault." Grayson's words were as soothing as the kiss. "I understand not getting it at first. I've had years to deal with the fact that Jax—

looking for it

I'm happy you see the situation from a new perspective. I'm happy it was you who made that decision. He may not come around so easily, but I fucking missed you, Sadie."

"I missed you too." I rose a little and stole another kiss. "I can't believe, all these years, I never thought what we did in front of the camera—"

"Was flirting? In a way, I'm glad, because it meant you never stopped."

I smiled. First real one in a few days. It felt incredible. "What about Jax?" Who I was almost certain now was listening.

"He's been waiting for you. And once he found out why you pushed him away…"

"He never told—" I clamped my jaw shut. He had told me how he felt. Several times. I ignored him, or threw it back at him for *teasing* me. I believed Chase had no idea back then what that one little lie would become, but it had shaped at least two lives for the next ten years. "I can't make things right if he won't talk to me."

Grayson grasped my fingers, tugged me to my feet, and wrapped an arm around my waist. He kissed me again, harder this time. It wasn't one of those ravenous, face-devouring kisses we'd shared before, but it was deep and intense, and I swore I felt his soul mingling with mine.

He pulled back and brushed a thumb over my bottom lip. "You already know he's in the other room, listening to everything."

"I guessed. How do I get him to talk to me?"

"He's still deciding if that's a good idea"—Jax's voice came from behind—"but watching you suck face with his boyfriend is forcing his hand."

What should have been playful words were carried on a stiff tone. If I couldn't make things right with Jax… I didn't know what I'd do.

Chapter Twenty-One

I turned, to see Jax lounging against the wall that led to the kitchen, his arms crossed. He was as heartachingly sexy as he'd always been.

It was tempting to keep dwelling on *so much wasted time*, but this was a chance to move forward. "It doesn't matter if you heard it all. I'll repeat it over and over, if you want," I said.

"The day you moved, when I propositioned you, I was surprised as fuck you said *yes*. You'd pushed me away for so long. It's nice to finally understand why." Jax's voice was thick with the same emotion clogging my throat. "I only asked for discretion because being out—any kind of *out* that people don't think is *normal*—is hard. When you didn't react well, Chase was a convenient excuse, but not one I should have used. Maybe if I'd pushed harder, at any point between then and now—"

"I wouldn't have reacted any better." We could play the *what if* game for days, around that one little thing that kept us apart. It wouldn't change anything. "I'm not concerned about what other people think.

My life is half on display anyway, and people can take their shitty judgments and go fuck themselves."

Jax smirked. I did adore that expression. "We've talked about you. A lot." He looked past me, to Grayson. "It was bad enough when one of us was smitten, but then he had to go and fall for you too."

"Smitten?" I loved it. Such a sweet, innocent word.

"Yes. And I understand your hesitation around being with both of us. When Grayson introduced me to the idea, way back when, I struggled with it too. Except it meant I could love him and not give up on you."

There was something in his words, the catch in his voice, that made my heart skip. I couldn't find a response.

Jax kicked away from the wall, walked up to me, and took my hand. "I tried to move on. Told myself it was pathetic that I couldn't get over a teenage crush. And I thought I had, until you were back in my life. Until Grayson, I never came close to feeling about anyone the way I did about you, and even now he lives in a separate place in my heart.

This wasn't *dating and seeing where things go*. He had a distinct destination in mind, and had for a while. I should be terrified or intimidated. Instead, I was settling into the relief that had been missing for weeks. "I'm sorry I believed the worst about you for

looking for it

so long. And that I don't have nearly as poetic a confession to make."

"That wasn't poetry, and all I need from you—ever—is the truth."

The truth. Should have been simple at any point along the way, but it always got muddled. Now it finally seemed so clear. "I'm glad you came back into my life. Chase's life, I guess. But he doesn't get any credit for this. Despite what I thought you'd done, I was happy to see you again. But I never dared think about you on that same level again. The hurt never left, and knowing now that it was misguided…" I wasn't going to tumble into hypotheticals. I had to remember that.

"You're committed to this idea now, of all of us?" Jax asked. "Because once you get past the hesitation, it feels really good, but you should know, it's hard falling for someone who already loves another person."

"I get that." I'd been getting that for years. "Believe me, I understand it implicitly."

Jax cradled my cheek against his palm. "Holding back all this time… Let's just say it's taught me infinite patience. But that day we hooked up, finally, the restraints snapped. I want you both, and I'm so happy you're good with that. I love you, Dee Dee."

I gazed back at amber eyes I used to think were cruel. Instead, he'd been as guarded as I was. "I hate that we wasted so much time." I had to say it. Voicing the regret made it easier to move past. "But we've got a lot of time ahead of us. And I love you too." Was I allowed to say that already? He said it first, and I meant it. Few things in my life felt more real or certain. Especially with Jax watching me in adoration, and Grayson wrapping his arms around my waist from behind.

Jax slid his hand to the back of my neck and crashed his mouth into mine. "I'm glad you wanted to do this here," he murmured between nibbles on my lips, "because we're not letting you leave for a few days."

I leaned into his kiss, letting the love and passion fill me. I turned to steal one from Grayson too. I'd almost walked away from this.

But I hadn't. That was what mattered.

Jax nudged my sweater up, and I stepped out of his grasp with a smile.

"It occurs to me"—or it was doing so as I spoke—"that having two boyfriends who are also dating each other means I get to watch you together." Which had recently become one of my favorite sights.

"What, specifically, do you want to watch?" Jax asked.

looking for it

I hadn't gotten into many details yet. My fantasies tended to focus more on my pleasure. That would be changing. "Kissing and nakedness and stuff?"

"All right." Jax sounded far too casual.

Grayson kissed him in a way I recognized—his fingers gripping the short strands of Jax's hair, their mouths dancing hungrily together.

It wasn't just the watching that sang to my soul, it was also knowing how it felt when Grayson did that. Being able to place myself in the middle of that kiss. And seeing how much they both enjoyed it.

There was no hesitating, only frantic desperation, as they stripped off each other's shirts. Bare, well-defined chests molded to each other. They groped one another through their jeans.

Jax made quick work of Grayson's belt and zipper. He slid his hands under Grayson's waistband, to grab Grayson's ass and pull him closer. The kissing never paused for more than a second or two.

Until Jax broke away, to drop to his knees. When he worked Grayson's cock free, I whimpered. It earned me a pair of twin smirks that faded when Jax took Grayson into his mouth.

I'd never been this turned on by something like porn. Grayson, fucking Jax's mouth. The intensity. The enthusiasm. The low groans that reached deep inside me and stroked my every nerve ending.

Grayson's hips thrust in time with breaths that grew shorter and shallower. "Stop." He forced the word through gritted teeth and pulled back from Jax, who stood.

Grayson turned to me, shaft at full mast, lust splashed across his face. "Come here."

I couldn't disobey an order like that. The instant I was within his reach, he grabbed my hips and kissed me hard. I swore something ripped with the desperation he used undoing my jeans.

He shoved my clothes to the ground, the fabric scraping along my thighs on the way down. "Being away from you for so many days"—his voice was strained—"turns out absence makes the dick grow harder."

"I'm pretty sure that's not how the saying goes." I laughed.

"I get to decide how things go," Grayson said. "For instance, kneel on the couch."

Yes, sir. I was barely settled, when he grabbed my hips, pushed me forward, and thrust his cock inside me. No fanfare, just *slam*, and *God*, I'd missed the way he stretched me out. I gripped the cushions to keep my balance, my head level with the back of the sofa. He slipped in and out of me at an excruciatingly slow pace, but each push forward was hard, striking the perfect spot inside me.

Then Jax was in front of me, cock in his hand. I hungrily took him in my mouth.

My hands were occupied, keeping me from falling over, but the guys seemed to have the other mechanics figured out. Grayson teased my clit, keeping up the slow rhythm of fucking me.

Jax wasn't so patient, thrusting against my face.

The combination of the words shared, the things I'd witnessed, and the sensations now drew a long climax from me. My cries were muffled by Jax's erection when I came.

A salty spurt hit the back of my throat, then another, as he spilled inside my mouth. I devoured every drop.

As Jax slipped past my lips, Grayson picked up the pace. Grunting. Pounding. Hammering against and inside me. The sounds he made when he reached climax were deliciously intoxicating.

The world slowed to a stop, punctuated by the three of us struggling to catch our breath. This wasn't soft sweetness, but the spice was incredible, and it was love. More amazing than I ever could have imagined.

Chapter Twenty-Two

There was no going out for coffee or running off to work the next morning. We did force ourselves to get out of bed for the essentials, around midday on New Year's Eve. Spent way too much time figuring out if all three of us could fit in their small tub, for a shower at the same time. We didn't manage, but the trying was a lot of fun.

And I absolutely knew what the pizza girl was thinking when Grayson answered the door in nothing but a pair of gray sweats.

While we were eating, Chase texted me, as he had every day for the past week.

"When are you going to answer him?" Grayson asked.

I hadn't decided yet. The anger wasn't there anymore, thanks largely to the fact it was hard to be angry about anything when I was sitting with my back against Jax's shoulder and my legs across Grayson's lap. "I'm letting him simmer."

Jax tugged my hair playfully. "A decade seems fair."

looking for it

"You haven't talked to him since Christmas?" Grayson managed to set his plate aside without disturbing my position. "You know he'd do anything for you."

"I haven't, and maybe next time he does something for me, he'll find out first if it's the thing I want."

"A person is allowed to learn and grow and change their mind." Grayson didn't even flinch at tossing my sentiment from yesterday back at me.

I stuck my tongue out at him. "Lying to and about people isn't the same as adjusting a perspective on how many people go in a relationship."

"Fair point." Grayson shrugged. "Then again, he didn't say it to or about me, so I'm not carrying the same kind of grudge."

Jax's barking laugh shook me. "Don't pull that bullshit. You were fuming after you heard what he'd done."

"It's true." Grayson lifted my legs and set my feet on the ground. "Speaking of Christmas— We never got to give you your gift. It wasn't in the stack at your parent's, because… we weren't sure anymore."

"We also haven't opened the ones from you yet. It didn't seem right," Jax said.

"What? You have to open them *now*." I'd forgotten about presents in middle of everything else, but now they could be a priority again.

Grayson kissed the palm of my hand. "Stay here."

He vanished into the other room and returned a moment later with a box that held two familiar wrapped packages. He handed Jax his, extracted his own, and set the box aside. "Who do you want to go first?"

Giddiness bubbled up. "It doesn't matter. Open them." It was a good thing neither of them were paper savers. I'd go nuts, watching them slowly cut around the tape.

I'd gotten Grayson a new set of headphones for streaming. He'd been eyeing them for months but kept putting off the purchase for one reason or another.

Jax's was a monogrammed leather portfolio, to hold documents for sales meetings. He gave me a curious look. "How did you...?"

"You said the one you carried was looking hammered." I was pleased they both liked their presents. The pair of hungry kisses I got as *thank yous* didn't hurt, either.

"Your turn." Jax reached over, to grab something else from the box. He extracted a small

looking for it

package, barely bigger than a business card, and only maybe an inch high.

My heart jammed in my throat. It was a jewelry box—that much was obvious from the size and shape. I'd never had a guy buy me jewelry before.

He handed me the gift. "Merry late Christmas."

The gold foil paper glittered in the light. If I tore into it, the surprise would be over, but I was also dying to see what was inside. I slipped a fingernail under one flap, slicing the tape neatly.

"Are you kidding me with that?" Grayson asked.

I laughed and tore off the rest of the paper. Inside, nestled on a bed of cotton, was a gold bracelet. It looked like three delicate ropes braided together. I lifted it out gently, processing how gorgeous it was. Two charms dangled from it—a pair of scissors with sapphires in the handles, and a circle that read *weapon of choice.*

"It's gorgeous," I said.

"Here." Grayson held out his hand.

I handed the bracelet over. He unclasped it and gently secured it on my wrist.

"I may never take it off. Thank you."

We spent the rest of the day with movies playing in the background, while we groped each other as much as we paid attention to what was on the screen. We fucked to the ball dropping and ringing in the New Year, and collapsed in a tangled-but-happy heap for the second night in the row.

The next morning, we took our time getting up, and there was discussion of me maybe heading home for a few hours, for a change of clothes and to prove to Lyn that I was still alive. For now, I was happy in one of Grayson's shirts and a pair of Jax's shorts.

We hadn't managed to leave the bedroom, when someone rang the doorbell.

"Be right back." Grayson squeezed my fingers and gave Jax a quick kiss before leaving to answer.

"Is my sister here?" I heard Chase's voice distinctly as it drifted in from the other room.

Jax nuzzled my neck. "Make him suffer a little longer, or grant him a reprieve?"

"Not sure." I was going to forgive Chase. Maybe in about five or ten minutes.

"Are you here?" Grayson hollered through the house.

I laughed and rolled my eyes. "Depends on who's asking," I yelled back.

"I'm not going to do this in a shouting match." Chase was doing exactly that.

"Try."

"I'm sorry." Chase's voice carried better than mine. That deep tenor had a commanding quality to it.

looking for it

Jax kissed the back of my neck and nudged me toward the door. As I stood, I grabbed his hand and tugged. "He owes you at least as much of an apology as he does me."

I recognized Chase's posture when we stepped into the living room. He had his back to the front door, and his arms were crossed. He looked me over, eyebrow raised. I stared back, unblinking.

"I'm sorry," he said again. "I didn't realize you'd held onto that, but I shouldn't have said it anyway. I was young. Stupid."

"*Was*? Past tense?" Jax said.

Chase snorted.

"Did you tell them to keep their grubby dicks off me?" I had to know. Because that wasn't nearly so long ago.

Chase nodded. "And they laughed at me for it."

Grayson moved to the side, so we could all see each other, and adopted a similar defensive posture to Chase's. "That's being kind."

"We told him to go fuck himself," Jax said.

Chase's shoulders drooped. He looked at all three of us again. There was no question *something* was going on, given my clothing. He didn't look upset. Not that his opinion would change my mind, but it would delay my forgiving him.

"They're good guys." Chase crammed his hands in his pockets. "I trust them implicitly, but you're more important. You're family. My baby sister, even if it is only by a year. If they make you happy… I can accept that. If that changes, I'll start smashing skulls."

Grayson rolled his eyes. "How very caveman of you."

"Yup." Chase gave me all his attention. "I'm sorry. I really am. To both of you. I can't take it back, but I know it was stupid."

"I get it. I forgive you. But if you do something like that ever again…" I was happy letting the unspoken threat hang in the air.

"That's fair." Chase crossed the room to wrap me in a tight hug. He stepped back and looked at Jax, questioningly.

Jax's sigh was exaggerated, and I had to fight a smile. "I guess we're cool." Jax only held his stony expression for a few seconds before it shattered into a smile.

Telling Mom and Dad needed to be even a quarter this easy.

We sent Chase on his way, and I headed home to grab a change of clothes and take a quick shower where flipping a coin to see if anyone got to share wasn't required. Not that I minded the playful struggle between who got to spend more time with whom.

looking for it

I was back at Jax and Grayson's place not long after. It wasn't as though I was moving in, but with Jax having the rest of the week off, and Grayson and me taking breaks from streaming, we were going to steal as much time together as we could.

Friday morning, I was surprised to see a phone call from an unknown number in California. "Hello?" I was prepared to hang up on a robodialer.

"Sadie? Hey, it's Chet Stanford."

My brain stumbled on the name, before catching up. "Yeah. Hi. I mean, how are you? How was your holiday?"

"Great. Look, I won't take a lot of your time, but I wanted talk to you sooner rather than later." He spoke more quickly than when we'd met in the courtesy suites, but he was just as friendly. "I'm sorry it took so long to get back to you. People have been in and out of the office all week, but I have the answers I hoped for."

I was missing something. "That's great?"

He laughed. "I missed a step. I do that when I'm excited. I loved your proposal, and so did the execs. We want to bring you on to do costume creation based on our specs, so our artists have something tangible to work from. But I needed a promise from Legal first that they could handle the fallout from the company pursuing you. They looked over your case, and they're going to take care of you."

I stared at Grayson and Jax, who were watching me with hopeful curiosity. Was this… It was the job I wanted. Creating for someone in public media. "Would I get artist credit?"

"Absolutely. And creative flexibility when it comes to making sure the designs are viable."

My name would be on video games. Asset sites. I'd get to make amazing new designs. I only saw one problem. "I'm not prepared to move to L.A. to do this." I had been a week ago, but my entire world had changed since then. Now Chet would tell me *never mind,* and I'd go back to that new life, missing the opportunity but knowing I couldn't leave my guys behind.

"That's okay. I didn't assume you'd want to," Chet said. "We will need you out here occasionally, to talk specs and look at what you come up with, but we're not equipped to have a seamstress in the building. This is a remote position."

"This sounds too good to be true." I meant to keep that to myself, but best to get it out now.

"I understand. I emailed you a contract. Look it over, take the weekend to think about it, and let me know."

"Yeah. Thank you." I couldn't think of anything else to say. I'd have questions once this sank in, but for now, I was basking in how amazing it sounded.

looking for it

I disconnected, relayed the brief conversation to Jax and Grayson, and was promptly showered with hugs and kisses.

The contract came through as promised.

Grayson read it aloud.

"You even make legalese sound sexy," I teased him. The offer was exactly what Chet promised. Grayson handed me back my phone, and I set it aside.

"Would you really have given up a chance like this for us?" he asked.

"Yes." I didn't hesitate. "I love you too much to walk away from what we're discovering. Both of you." I hadn't said that specifically to Grayson yet, but the words felt incredible. "I love you so much."

He kissed me on the forehead. "I love you too. I'm glad you figured it out before it was too late."

"Arrogant asshole." I reached to smack him playfully, and he grabbed my wrist.

Heat rushed through me at the intensity in his gaze and the possession in his grip.

Jax pressed his lips to my neck, right below my ear. "What round will this be?"

"I'm not keeping count." I leaned back into him.

This was amazing. Whatever came next, we were ready for it. All three of us together, the way it should be.

Epilogue

August was the perfect time for a wedding. I was grateful to not be restricted to something like *saving myself for the wedding night*, but heading our separate ways had gotten harder and harder as the months passed by.

And for the last few weeks, I'd been too busy with wedding prep to spend much time with Jax and Grayson. Even with Anne and Lyn stepping in to help with the big things, my calendar had been full. Partly with finishing my wedding dress, which the guys hadn't seen yet.

I stood in what wouldn't be my bedroom after today, in Lyn's house, smoothing out the gown and studying my reflection.

"You look gorgeous." Anne tucked a loose strand of hair into the pins holding my updo in place. My hair wasn't quite long enough for a fancy style, but she'd given me ringlets and made my currently pale-pink tresses into a plaited design any woman would envy.

looking for it

My hair color matched the embroidery and pearls I'd sewn into my gown. Lace hugged my torso, hips, and legs, and stretched into a short train behind me. It wasn't the princess dress that child-me imagined. It was stunning and elegant.

Lyn and Anne had similar style dresses, but in rich green and blue respectively, and minus the trains. I'd used the excess satin from my dress to make handkerchiefs for the guys' suits. Chase insisted I give him a blue one.

"Are you nervous?" Anne fidgeted with her skirt and shifted her weight from one foot to the other.

"Yeah. Not in a bad way. Like… I can't believe this is happening, you know?"

She grinned. "I do know. Me too."

Someone knocked, and she hurried to open the door.

My dad stood on the other side. "Are you ready?" He and Mom had barely flinched when I told them I was dating two men, especially when they found out who those men were. I'd taken the opportunity to point out to Chase that made him more uptight than our parents.

I nodded. "I'm ready." I wanted this to be over with, and at the same time, I wanted to savor every second of today.

Anne gave me a quick hug. "I'll see you downstairs." She hurried away, to take her place in the wedding procession.

Lyn was loaning us her house for the day, including her kitchen and back yard. She'd wanted to cater as well, but I made her promise if she cooked, she had to be done before the wedding, and someone else had to do the serving and the work. I wanted her and Anne by my side through this.

I descended the back stairs with Dad, and heard the electric organ kick up with the wedding march. The marriage wasn't state sanctioned or anything; we wouldn't have an official license for the three of us. But we'd have the ceremony and the promises we made here, and that meant everything to me.

When we stepped out the back door, I couldn't see anything but Jax and Grayson waiting for me at the altar. Their faces lit up. They were my entire universe. The best thing that ever happened to me.

I was on autopilot during the pastor's introduction. I managed my vows only because I'd practiced them a million times in front of the mirror. The rings Jax and Grayson gave me had been made to intertwine with each other, and I couldn't think of anything more appropriate as a symbol of our love.

The preacher said they could kiss the bride, and the both planted chaste kisses on my cheeks.

looking for it

Then Grayson captured my face and pressed his mouth to mine, in a long, drawn-out vow that was the perfect seal to our recited words.

Jax cleared his throat, and stole me away for his own kiss. I was pretty sure people were cheering and clapping, but my new husbands were the only thing in my world right now.

Jax pressed his forehead to mine. "If you're leaving that mattress behind, we've got one last chance to abuse it before the reception starts," he whispered.

I grinned. "Let's do it."

This was nothing like what I'd dreamed of when I built my perfect-life plan. It was so much better, and I was looking forward to every single minute of it.

About Allyson Lindt

USA Today Bestselling Author Allyson Lindt is a full-time geek and a fuller-time author. She's found her own happily ever after, where she and her spouse call their furbabies their children. Coffee is her task-master and random tangents are her muse. When she's not writing, she's fangirling over the latest superhero movies. She likes her stories with sweet geekiness and heavy spice, and loves a sexy happily-ever-after. Because cubicle dwellers need love too. Learn more about Allyson's books, including signing up for her newsletter, by visiting http://www.allysonlindt.com.